WARNING: this story contains a lot of swearing (many f-bombs), violence, and sexual content.

Intended for readers 18+

Born To Be Wicked

(Book 1 of the Demon Employment series)

Born To Be Wicked – Book 1
Born To Be Devilish – Book 2
Born To Be Badass – Book 3

Shade Owens
www.shadeowens.com

Edited by Nikki Busch
www.nikkibuschediting.com

RED RAVEN PUBLISHING

© Copyright 2021 Shade Owens
ISBN: 978-1-990271-37-3

Chapter 1

"He's getting away," comes Jamieson's rugged voice in my ear.

His English accent is sexy, but that doesn't make us friends.

I press the little speaker in my ear and nod as if he can see me. He can't, but I don't give a shit. Right now, all I care about is my $50,000 mark leaving the party.

This job is huge. I can't mess it up. Besides, this evening gown wasn't easy to get. If I don't finish the job, threatening the store clerk's life will have all been for nothing.

My mark's name is Adam Shaw—a young billionaire who inherited daddy's company and now makes his dollars off the backs of others. It's my job to know about my mark, and even more so when it comes to a guy like Adam. Everyone knows him, which is why the payout is so damn big. To prepare for this, I've spent months researching everything I can about the guy, so I'll be damned if he slips through my fingers because of some unforeseen situation.

"Don't fuck this up, Alexis."

I'm about to tell Jamieson to shut that rotten hole in his face, but he's my boss. He can treat me however he wants if it means I get to pay my bills for another few months.

Adam Shaw exits the hall through the main entrance, his posture as stiff as a piece of plywood. He moves around like he owns the place... which, technically, he does. Still. It makes him look like a jackass. His hair, a clean shave on either side, is a yellow blond that almost looks transparent under the overhead lights. The top of his hair is combed back and gelled with something so organic millennials would probably line up for hours to get a good sniff of it.

"Have a great night, Mr. Shaw," says one of the guards at the front.

Adam smirks back at him—an attractive smile that he's totally practiced a thousand times in front of his overpriced mirrors. He wraps his black-sleeved arm around the stunning woman standing next to him.

She's the problem... she's getting in the way. The plan was to seduce Adam myself and take him home, but everyone knows that Adam Shaw's a playboy. I knew there was a possibility that another girl would get to him before I did.

While I rarely lose sleep if innocent feebles get in the way—that's lingo for nonmagical people and admittedly derogatory—I do my best to avoid hurting anyone who isn't involved.

This girl isn't involved, and I don't want to hurt her, but I need to get the job done. Adam's closest bodyguard, Mo Thompson, left for a trip to the Bahamas two hours ago. The man replacing him is on the men's restroom floor, knocked out from the tranquilizer I injected in his neck.

Didn't see that coming, did ya tough guy?

Adam Shaw turns around, likely wondering where his trusted protector is, but it's obvious getting laid is more important than trying to figure out his bodyguard's whereabouts. That's Adam's downfall—he thinks he's untouchable with his guards, his security system, and his money.

What he doesn't know is that while he was celebrating his recent business achievement here, I hacked into his home's security system and deactivated everything.

Placing my glass of chardonnay down on one of the server's trays, I rush through tall marble columns and down a narrow passageway that leads to the side exit of the building.

This is my job.

I'm good at it.

Not only did I pull up blueprints for all of Adam Shaw's house, I also studied this conference center's entire architectural structure before doing my hair this evening.

My heels tick as I run, so I tear them off midway,

my feet slapping against the cold floor. From a distance, I hear the sound of a car's beep, which is the exact sound made by the one and only sky blue Bugatti Chiron Adam owns.

Everyone knows it's his; no one else in the city drives a car that expensive.

That means he's about to get in.

Bolting around the side of the building, I charge straight toward his car. His engine rumbles and his headlights turn on, looking like two prison spotlights in the dark.

Shit.

I need to move faster.

Running as fast as I can, I lunge at his front hood. The surprise is enough for him to slam on his brakes, causing his shiny black tires to squeal across the pavement. My body smashes hard against his perfectly waxed hood, and in a less-than-graceful posture, I roll up his windshield, over his roof, and straight into the air.

I knew what I was getting into, but that doesn't make the impact any less unpleasant.

My arm snaps and my left shoulder dislocates, but that's not what bothers me—I cringe at the sight of the tear in my dress that looks irreparable.

Son of a bitch.

Behind his car, I now lie flat on my back, his exhaust fumes polluting my lungs.

Around me, dozens of people gasp like a flock of seagulls circling a loaf of bread. One old man limps toward me in a hurry, the few strands of hair on his head holding on for dear life as he runs through an evening breeze.

"Oh my goodness... Are you all right, miss?"

Typically, I wouldn't have made such a drastic move to get my mark. My job is to remain as discreet as possible, and getting hit by Adam's car is enough to lead the police to believe I had a motive to take him out.

But I spent months preparing for tonight, and I'll be damned if some little Barbie doll keeps me from earning my $50,000 paycheck. Jobs like these don't come around too often, and with how I've been managing my money lately, well... I could use the extra cash.

Turning my face away from the crowd, I snap my broken bone back into place and pop my shoulder into its socket.

"I'm fine," I mumble, refusing to show the man my face.

"Are... are you sure?" comes his old, quivering voice.

While I appreciate the kindness, I can't be seen.

"I said I'm fine," I hiss, and my succubus horns nearly tear out of my skull.

Adam jumps out of his car, his thick brows meeting over the narrow bridge of his nose. Instead of coming around back to check on me, he hurries to the front of his car and inspects for damage by delicately grazing his metallic baby.

Oh, how I'm going to enjoy tonight.

"What's wrong with you?" he snaps, now storming around his vehicle.

He must have found a dent.

Good.

Maybe I should have left my broken arm, well, broken. Would that have stirred up even an ounce of remorse in him? Should I pretend to be hurt? Should I cry?

Alexis Rayne doesn't cry.

In fact, I can't even recall the last time I genuinely cried, which is saying a lot given that I'm over a thousand years old. I'm the epitome of a succubus—strong, dominant, and seductive.

He moves toward me, his features contorted so profoundly that I'm tempted to dig my claws around his hairline and pull back. Maybe a facelift will eradicate that hideous scowl of his.

Instead, I slap my hand on the trunk of his car and use it as support as I bring myself onto my feet. As I get up, I push a little harder than necessary on his car, causing his suspension to squeak. It pisses him off, which is what I was hoping for. I may be a powerful demon capable of snapping his neck like a twig, but watching him get all worked up is so much more enjoyable.

"What the fuck, lady?" he shouts.

My left eyelid flutters as I fight the urge to dig my claws into the metal of his car. As much as it would satisfy me, I'll never reveal my true self in front of feebles. If anyone finds out I'm fae—or a demon, as many like to call me—I'll be forced to get my identity changed once again, which is beyond exhausting.

Pushing my succubus self back inside, I stare him cold in the face.

"Are you okay, young lady?" someone asks.

"Did you see that?"

"How is she standing?"

"Are you okay?"

Impatient, I wave a hand at the crowd of people who remind me of crows around a dead carcass.

"I'm fine."

"Are you sure?"

"I said I'm—" but I cut myself short, feeling Red build up.

My new therapist tells me to call my anger Red. Apparently, that gives my anger a persona, which makes it easier for me to control. I'm also told I have a need to control things. When Red builds up, I risk being unable to suppress my demon self, and the last thing I need is for innocent bystanders to see me full-on succubus—sharp blue eyes, long platinum-white hair, black horns, and massive dragon-like wings.

If that ever gets out, I'll be done for. Jamieson's made it clear that he doesn't work with shadow dwellers—a term given to nonfeebles (fae, vampires, witches). Some shadow dwellers hate the term because it insinuates we should remain in hiding, but heck, I kind of like it. It's dark, mysterious, and sexy.

Jamieson doesn't know what I am, and he can't find out, either.

Inhaling a long slow breath, I calm my heart rate despite Adam Shaw's hateful gaze. He's shouting something, though I'm not listening. I don't give a shit what he has to say. His thick lips flap up and down and his hands wave in front of my face.

That's when I let it happen.

My Lure.

I smile at him, waiting for the tantrum to stop. Immediately, his big blue eyes soften and he stops talking, clears his throat, and tugs at his tuxedo's collar.

"I... um," he stammers. "I'm so sorry. How about I take you back to my place and get you all cleaned up? I'll replace your dress. I'll pay you. Whatever you want. You deserve the best treatment."

He stares at my chest, my lips, and then my eyes again.

Smirking, I raise my chin and stare back.

"Are you fucking kidding me?" comes a woman's shrill voice.

His date storms out of the car, slamming the door behind her, and marches straight toward me. Her dress, a silk red sheet held in place by two cordlike straps, accentuates her petite but curvy shape. The deep V-cut on her chest reveals two perfectly round, supple breasts that are most definitely natural.

Biting my lower lip, I take her all in.

"Who do you think you are?" she snaps, dropping her leather purse to the ground. She scowls, no doubt preparing to ream me out, but the moment she makes eye contact with me, her jaw snaps shut.

"I, um—" she mumbles.

Slowly, I scan her body with narrowed eyes, admiring the perfection in her curves. Beside her, Adam fidgets with his thumbs and clears his throat. Something tells me that if I don't do this quickly, he might get aggressive and jump me.

It wouldn't be the first time that happened. If I throw my Lure at a victim for too long, they can't handle it and shit gets intense. I'd be lying if I said I minded it. At the end of the day, I'm more powerful than any feeble, so if having their way with me is what rings their bell, I'm willing.

You want me to devour you? I say in my mind.

I don't make a habit of talking to my prey when they're entranced, but in certain situations, it works wonders. They don't hear me, per se—it's more of a brainwashing technique than anything.

Tilting my head, I bite my nail. "I'm sorry about your car."

"No, no," Adam says quickly.

His date chimes in, her eyes never leaving my chest. "Oh, please. It's no problem at all. Why don't you, um, come with us? We'll get you... cleaned up."

This wasn't the plan.

Adam's the mark, not her. But I'm too far in, and if I plan to finish the job, I can't stop now. Besides, I don't want to stop now.

I'm too hungry.

I elevate my chin. "Well, what are you waiting for? Let's go."

Chapter 2

We don't even make it into Adam's bedroom.

The moment we step into his multimillion-dollar mansion, he grabs me by the waist and lifts me into the air. I wrap my legs around his body and hold on tight.

You want me, bad boy?

"I fucking want you." He breathes hard like he's high on something.

Dragging the tips of my concealed claws against the back of his skull, I lick the side of his neck, tasting primal excitement mixed with crisp, high-end cologne.

"God, I want you," he says again.

This time, he grabs me by the back of my hair and forces my lips against his. His breath, hot and minty, fills my mouth.

He carries me into his living room, his lips never leaving mine. The room is massive—easily the size of an exclusive shopping boutique—but I'm too preoccupied with all the kissing to inspect the interior of his house. Besides, I already know what it looks like in here.

I could even tell you where he keeps his coffee mugs, or where his housekeeper stores her cleaning supplies, but those details are irrelevant.

All I care about is feeding.

He throws me onto his white leather couch, his chest heaving and the veins of his neck popping out. With legs crossed and my arms spread out on the backrest behind me, I watch him.

So *pathetic*, I think to myself.

He grunts a bunch of nonsense, then tears off his shirt and desperately tries to unbuckle his belt. At the same time, his date rushes to her knees in front of him, her cheeks as rosy as his.

They're so entranced by my Lure that they'll do anything for me—all I have to do is tell them what I want.

"Untie it," I order, and the woman tears so hard on Adam's belt that his hips sway back and forth. When it unclips, she yanks the belt out, the leather making a sharp hissing sound.

Smiling, I rub my neck, my chest, and my thighs.

Adam's hungry eyes roll my way as his date reaches inside his briefs. While he may be enjoying her hot breath against him, what he wants is me.

I get up, the sound of my heels echoing throughout his house. As I make my way around him, he watches my every movement like the pathetic dog he is. He closes his eyes and shudders when I drag my fingernails across his forearm, extracting speckles of blood.

He's never wanted anything so badly in his life before.

I press my lips against his neck, his shoulders, and his back. Grazing his warm skin with my lips, I make my way back to his earlobe. "How bad do you want me, Adam?"

He's too entranced to respond. Instead, he nods as thousands of goose bumps erupt all over his body. He swallows hard, his throat sticking, and stops breathing when I press my breasts against his back. Slowly, I wrap my fingers around his neck, feeling his heart pulsate in his carotid artery.

He wants to be dominated—most feebles do when I'm working my Lure.

I tighten my grip around his throat.

"What do you want, Adam?" I say.

"Y-y-you," he stammers.

"Would you do anything for me, Adam?"

"Y-y-yes," he moans. "I'd do anything for you."

With fangs bared behind him, I press the tips of my claws into his neck but stop myself before I sever his head in front of his date. With how hypnotized he is, I could easily tell Adam to get a gun and blow his brains out. He'd do it, but what fun would that be? I'm hungry, and I'll be damned if I waste a decent meal.

"I want you to do something for me," I say.

"Anything," he says, his eyes rolling back as his date pleasures him.

"Sit down and watch," I order.

I push his date away from him and Adam moves to the couch like a robot and sits his bare butt down.

The woman, seemingly confused, glances up at me.

"Get up," I order.

She does as she's been told and stands up, her eyes glazed over.

Without allowing her to see my claws, I reach for her dress's right shoulder strap and I slice through it. It slips off her shoulder like rainwater through a downspout and falls around her smooth naked belly full of goosebumps.

"That's better," I say.

She wants to speak, but she's too hypnotized to think.

"It's okay," I say, pressing a finger against her lips. "You don't need to speak."

Slowly, I lead her backward until her legs catch the sofa and she falls into a seated position.

"Lie down," I say, and she lies across the sofa with one arm above her head. I can hear her racing heart from where I stand. This woman has wanted nothing more than this in her entire life.

Smiling, I climb on top of her and kiss her neck, her jaw, her chest.

"What do you want?" I breathe, my tongue sliding down her abdomen.

"You," she moans.

While I'd much prefer to play with my food before feeding, I don't have the luxury of time. When I'm on a mission, my goal is to get the job done.

I tease her for a bit, but it's obvious she can't handle it. She grabs my hair, pulling my body closer to hers, and I turn my face sideways to spot Adam on the sofa, watching us with wild passion in his eyes.

With my mind, I order Adam to join us, and the room gets hot.

Everything feels so fucking amazing.

For a moment, I forget that I'm working a mission. Sex as a succubus and with a succubus is a mind-blowing sensation that can only be described as euphoric. Those who have survived to tell about it often equate it to having sex on ecstasy... tenfold.

As things get intense, I lower my fangs close to his date's neck. I may not be a vampire, but sex brings out the most primal side of me. It takes everything in me not to hurt someone during mealtime. I need to consciously remind myself that my teeth and my claws are powerful enough to kill a feeble.

The biting and the tearing of skin are reserved for fae only.

The two feebles release moans of pleasure as we get closer to my feeding time.

Finally.

The ecstasy.

I pull away and smile down at the woman's red face. Her eyes roll up at me, but it's like she doesn't even see me, which is typically what happens after sex with a succubus—my victims fall into a drug-like state. She beams as if this was her first time, but the joyous look on her face doesn't last long, and I know why—my true self is coming out.

After sex, I can't help it; my succubus can't be contained.

Out of my head come curved black horns, and out of my back, massive dragon-like wings. My long black hair lightens to a platinum white, and my blue eyes do the same.

The look of horror on her face makes me feel guilty, but I can't control my urge to feed. Cupping her jaw with my claws, I lower my lips against hers and breathe in deep, pulling from her mouth an indigo purple mist. As it fills me, I'm energized.

There's no feeling in the world more satisfying than feeding. If I were to describe it, I would equate it to the feeling feebles might experience when I fuck them.

For her, however, my feeding causes the opposite effect.

Her skin lightens in color until it looks as though she's on the verge of decaying. Her eye sockets sink as squiggly black lines run across her skin, her neck, and her chest.

"What the fuck—" comes Adam's voice.

If I don't stop now, I'll kill her. But she tastes so goddamn good. I suck harder and harder as her cheeks begin to cave. I may have learned to control myself, but stopping midfeed isn't something that gets easier over time. Though I'm not proud of it, I've slipped up a few times in the last decade.

She isn't your mark, Alexis. Adam is.

Suddenly, I'm reminded that I have a real meal at my disposal.

Digging my claws into the sofa's cushion, I pull away. Her lifeless eyes roll into the back of her head as she falls into a comatose state. There's no telling when she'll recover. Sometimes, it takes hours, though I've seen feebles require several days for a full recovery.

What matters is that she won't remember any of this.

"What... What are you?" says Adam.

I turn around, my wings sweeping through the air. At the sight of my demon self, he stumbles backward, his skin blanched.

He stares at me, mortified, and before he has the chance to figure out what's going on, I throw myself at him. Our lips lock, and I inhale his life force. It fills me up, energizing me completely. When I finish feeding, his head rolls to the side and he gazes into nothingness.

Mission complete.

And holy fuck do I feel amazing.

I jump up with a bounce and make my way over

to the small purse I dropped earlier in Adam's foyer. From it, I extract an earpiece and spy camera, which I tucked away en route to Adam's house. Jamieson doesn't get to see how I go about doing my business—all he gets to know is *when* I locate my mark and confirmation that the job's been done.

Turning the camera on, I crouch next to Adam's dead body and aim it at his face. Then, I spin my lip ring—a secret microphone—and say, "Target down."

"How'd you pull that off?" Jamieson says through my earpiece.

I turn off the camera. "How many times do we have to go over this?"

I'm being polite. We've talked about this many times, and what I want to say is, *Would you stop fucking asking me that?* I don't ask him questions about who he wants taken out, and he doesn't ask me questions about my methods. All he gets is a one-second glimpse of the dead body for confirmation.

"All right, all right," he says. "Good work, Alexis. I'd say thank you, but I think you're the one who should be thanking me."

God, he's such a jackass. What does he want? For me to climb on his lap and call him *Daddy*? Thank him for giving me such an incredible opportunity? I'm not that kind of woman. I was asked to do a job, and I did it. Sure, I want the money, but he needs me as much as I need him.

"Contact me when you have another job," I say, and before he gets the chance to slide in another snarky remark, I twist my lip ring to turn off my microphone.

Chapter 3

I flick the syringe a few times to get the bubbles out and stick the needle into Adam's median cubital vein—the big blue vein inside his elbow. Inside this syringe is a lethal dose of heroin, which means when the cops find his body, they won't suspect foul play. Instead, they'll think he overdosed.

His date gets the second injection, but hers is microdosed. It's a tactic I've been using for several years now, and it hasn't failed me yet. Not only will she not remember who I am, but on the microscopic chance that she remembers a third party being present, well... her testimony won't be reliable. No one's going to trust a witness who was on heroin the night of Adam's death.

I stretch my neck to the side, a satisfying snap echoing across Adam's mansion.

"Look at this place," I say aloud. "You're one rich son of a bitch."

I glance over at Adam's lifeless body, knowing he isn't going to respond.

As I examine his house with curious fascination,

I realize I could earn a lot more than $50,000. Should I feel bad for robbing a dead guy? Of course not. He was an asshole. Besides, I'm a murderer. Being a thief on top of it won't make me any more of a criminal.

I cross his dining room and enter his kitchen, jealous of his enormous fridge.

A thing like that could fit hundreds of beers.

I'm about to make my way into his bedroom—the one place I know he keeps countless brand name watches—when I spot a bottle of 1952 Dragon's Tear whiskey. It sits enticingly, its rich golden hue shimmering beneath the kitchen's overhead light. The bottle is shaped like a dragon with an ornate tail twirling around its body.

That limited-edition whiskey sells for over $60,000, but that's not what has me slack-jawed. What confuses me is that everyone knows that vampires own the distillery that produces this stuff, and they're uptight about who's allowed to purchase it. So why does Adam have a bottle sitting in plain sight? It's been said that the alcohol isn't intended for feebles... they aren't even supposed to know about it. Some people have even said it was distilled using feeble blood.

I peer into the living room at Adam's colorless body, wondering if maybe my senses are off. As of late, they have been. Is he fae? He can't be. I've been following him for months.

I know my mark, but... what if I missed

something?

Closing my eyes, I inhale a deep breath.

There's no scent of fae whatsoever here, but something's up. Without thinking, I snatch the bottle and make my way upstairs and into his bedroom. Placing the bottle of whiskey down on his mahogany dresser, I slide my fingers across the very same box I've seen him open numerous times during those nights I observed him from his bedroom window.

His watches.

Adam may have been a dick, but he wasn't a moron. This box isn't simply a storage box—it's a safe, which means I can't take it and run. As I stare at it, wondering how I might go about taking the watches without leaving any indication of a robbery, I catch a glimpse of myself in his bedroom mirror.

My torn dress clings to my body, and my long black hair drapes down my back. While I may be beautiful on the outside, I'm still adjusting to my new appearance. Taking a step toward the mirror, I reach for the pale skin of my cheek and stare into my sky blue eyes.

I've changed appearances so many times I'm losing sight of who I am.

Three years ago, when I became Alexis Rayne, I let go of my wavy blond hair and green eyes along with a city I'd come to think of as home. I lay in bed for weeks following my morph. Despite how many times I've tried to explain to my best friend, Draxomus (I call him Drax), that morphing my physical appearance takes an immeasurable amount of strength, it's as if he thinks I'm exaggerating, and that no matter what happens, I'll always be able to change my appearance, my name, and my town.

While he may not have minded uprooting his entire life and starting anew in a different city, it was one of the hardest things I've had to do in over a century.

I stare at my reflection, thinking back to my old life and my old home tucked away on Aspen Private at the center of Jormane—a small town on the outskirts of San Halos. As I tour my home within my memories, it isn't my rich red oak flooring I think about, nor my $10,000 leather sofas.

What lingers in my mind are colorful crayons spread out across the kitchen tiles, sketches posted on the refrigerator, a lunchbox sitting on the kitchen island, and laughter bouncing off the walls as Mr. Mushroom prances around with a small sneaker in his mouth.

What I wouldn't give to go back in time.

Sighing, I turn away from the mirror, grab the bottle of Dragon's Tear whiskey, and crack it open. As I tilt it, the fluid slips down my throat, burning my insides, and a sense of relief washes over me.

I may be breaking my own rule by drinking on the job, but the job's finished, and the only thing I want is to *not feel* my pain. I want to forget.

I pace back and forth in Adam's bedroom as the alcohol burns my throat, focusing my energy on figuring out how to break through his safe without leaving evidence behind. I may not have fingerprints anymore—I burned them off in the late eighteen hundreds when investigators started using forensic science to identify criminals—but I'm a professional, and I refuse to leave any evidence that may cause suspicion. I've never been one to worry about my hair falling out; my succubus DNA always turns up inconclusive. Feebles don't realize it, but demons are often the reason so many murder cases become cold. Our DNA doesn't show up the way feeble DNA does, which makes it impossible to track us down.

As the alcohol swims through my blood and my inhibition fades, I stare at the safe full of watches.

Would it be so bad to smash it and run?

What do you care, Alexis? It's not like they'll trace any of this back to you. No one saw you come to Adam's house. You were careful. Besides, these watches, along with Jamieson's paycheck, could get you out of your shitty apartment.

Fuck it.

I crack my neck, form a fist, and smash the top of the small safe. The wood snaps and the metal of the box warps, leaving a space between the lid and the frame.

The joys of having super strength.

With my index finger, I widen the crack of the box until the lid snaps off. Inside are a red velvety material and six glistening watches—all of which look more expensive than Adam's car.

F. P. Journe.

Richard Mille.

Vacheron Constantin.

Holy fuck. These watches are worth thousands.

I slip my claws through each watch and shake my wrists until they slide down my forearms.

"Thanks, Adam," I mumble, grabbing the bottle of whiskey by the neck.

With a wobble in my walk, I head toward the bedroom window and pull at the latch. It doesn't open, which makes me feel like a total idiot. Am I *that* drunk? I tug again, and this time, something clicks.

The problem is that the window is still locked, which means the clicking sound didn't come from the latch.

The sound of someone clearing their throat resonates behind me.

I swing around, Adam's watches clinging against each other on my wrists, only to find myself standing face-to-face with a man carrying an automatic rifle. He stares at me from behind the gun's barrel, his eyes dark and menacing. His hair, a cool jet black, sits messily atop his head, matching the short unkempt scruff on his face. Black tribal tattoos run down his neck, his arms, and even his knuckles.

"Who the fuck are you?" he asks, a thick gangster accent rolling off the tip of his tongue.

I'm tempted to try to seduce him, but with how much alcohol I consumed, it might interfere with my powers. What the hell was I thinking? This is why I don't drink on the job. Shit can get messy.

He jerks his gun in the air as if to say, *Well?*

I could attack him and tear off his head, but I don't exactly feel like getting shot in the face, even if I'm immortal. So, I do the one thing I can think of. With the bottle of whiskey gripped in my hand, I dive headfirst through Adam's bedroom window. Glass shards explode all around me as I tumble from his second story, but right before I land in his perfectly trimmed courtyard, I spin my body around, expand my wings, and blast myself toward the full moon.

CHAPTER 4

"You shouldn't have taken those," Drax says like he's my dad.

Rolling my eyes, I flick my wrists, sending Adam's watches flying onto my living room sofa. "I don't need a lecture, Drax. The guy was filthy rich. Look at me—" I swing my arm out, pointing at the inside of my apartment. "Don't you think it's only fair that I get some of those riches?"

My apartment looks like something that was thrown together using materials found in an overflowing garbage bin. The walls are torn to shit. In certain spots, drywall is missing entirely and in its place are insulation and wooden support beams. My couches are probably a century old (that's a bit of an exaggeration, and I would know) with their frayed cushions and ugly mismatched colors. My floors, nasty yellow parquet wood, are so chipped and scratched you'd think I keep a lion here as a pet.

The floor damage is my fault, though. I've spent more drunken nights than I can count throwing anger fits with my succubus claws out. Okay—the shitty apartment is also my fault. I haven't exactly been careful with my money lately.

In one hand, out the other.

Drax shakes his green-skinned head and slaps a hand on his forehead. It's obvious he wants to give me shit, and if I were to guess, he probably wants to say, *Well, maybe if you didn't drink so fucking much and spend your money God knows where...* but Drax's too nice for that. Instead, he says, "That's not the point, Alex. The police are gonna be all over this. Adam wasn't some no-name. You should be keeping your head low. And holding on to a bunch of his watches that only someone like that prick could afford won't do you any favors. It's not like you can sell them right now, anyway."

I scoff. "Why not? You think some black market criminal gives a shit where I got these from?"

Drax stares at me the way he always does after I finish a job—a look that says, *Why do you tell me everything if all you're going to do is shit all over my advice?*

Part of me knows it's stupid to talk to him about my marks, but he's like a brother to me and I trust him with my life. He isn't much older than I look, which is like a thirty-year-old despite my true age, but sometimes he treats me as if he were my dad.

I don't blame him—I've caused this. I haven't exactly been myself lately.

"Would you stop looking at me like that?" I say.

Tightening his lips, he refuses to look away and instead narrows his yellow eyes and plays with his right horn.

Drax is fae, too, or more specifically, a reptilian humanoid. He's slender with scaly skin, and sticking out of his forehead are two small brown horns that look like something off an unusually small water buffalo. His nose isn't even a nose—instead, two nostrils sit on his face like a snake's. Underneath his smeller are sharp carnivorous teeth that make him look pretty freaky when he smiles. It's a good thing feebles can't see fae in their true forms. If they did, they'd likely die of a heart attack.

But I know Drax—he's a nice guy. So nice, in fact, that his entire demon family cast him out as a kid for not wanting to eat children. If there's one line I won't cross, it's kids. That, and animals. I'll slit a guy's throat and make him drink his own blood as he dies, but lay a hand on a dog? Hurt a cat? No way. I've killed more guys than I can count for abusing their dogs, and I didn't even get paid for that shit.

I didn't seduce them first, either. It was more of a kidnapping and torturing situation, but I won't get into that. Otherwise, you'll see me as a monster. And I wouldn't want that.

One time, I caught a crazy bitch throwing cans of soup at her dog's face. Well, I turned her face into soup and took the dog.

Mr. Mushroom, no doubt sensing that I'm thinking about that awful day, jumps up onto my lap and licks my face. He's a beige French bulldog, and yes, I named him after the soup incident; they were cans of mushroom soup. What can I say?

"Hey, little man." I scratch him along his snout with my index finger. He pants and grins, revealing a slobbery pink tongue. I grab the loose skin of his face and playfully tug at it, but stop myself before my *cute aggression* (it's a thing, look it up) takes over and makes me pull too hard. Instead, I breathe out through flared nostrils and kiss him hard on the forehead. "God, I could eat your face!"

Drax looks at me like I've morphed into my full succubus self.

"Until you have a dog, keep your opinions to yourself," I say.

He blinks. "I've had plenty of dogs, including Lilac. You know I lost her last month."

"Oh, right," I say, feeling slightly insensitive.

Drax plops down on the couch across from me and stares at the watches between us.

"Something's up," he says.

Drax knows me too well. Maybe if I say nothing, he'll let it go. I kick my feet up onto the table, causing the pile of watches to bounce, and close my eyes.

Something soft smashes me in the face.

"What the—"

Drax glares at me with another cushion held up

next to his face. "Something's wrong, Alex. You gonna spill, or am I gonna have to hit you again?"

When Drax gets the couch cushions involved, I know he means business. Besides, he's right—something *is* up, and that something is the guy who saw me at Adam's place.

How did this even happen? I've never had a witness before. The few times I was spotted, well… I took care of it. But now, someone out there knows who I am and knows what I did. Why did I run? Why didn't I try to kill him? Fucking whiskey. I need to pull myself together. It was a moment of stupidity and I feel like a complete idiot for how things went down. I'm supposed to be tougher than this. I'm supposed to be a professional.

"Alex," he says, slanting his hairless eyebrows.

Shrugging, I point at the bottle of Dragon's Tear on the coffee table between us. "You should try it."

"How the hell did you get your hands on that?" A hint of excitement flashes across his face. "Some people say the buzz is like—" Likely realizing that this isn't the time to get excited, he straightens his posture and clears his throat. "What does this have to do with anything? You must've fucked up royally if you think I need to be inebriated for you to tell me what happened."

Without looking up at him, I say, "Someone saw me."

His eyes pop out—and when I say pop out, I mean *pop* out. Maybe it's the reptilian in him… It's almost as if some hidden frog ancestry comes out when something startles him.

"Who? Who saw you, Alex?" He leans forward, dropping his elbows on his knees. "Where? In the house? Did they say anything? Was it a guy? A girl?"

His interrogation isn't helping my stress level. If anything, it's making me want to light a smoke, and I quit three months ago. Not for health reasons, but because I was sick of waking up drunk with the taste of cigarettes in my mouth.

I'll be damned if all my hard work was for nothing. With a swing of the arm, I snatch the Dragon's Tear off the table, crack it open, and take a swig. As I breathe out, the smell of whiskey fills my nostrils and a sense of calm washes over me. "I don't know who it was. Maybe his bodyguard. Maybe his fucking drug dealer. I don't know. I jumped out the window."

His jaw hangs loose, revealing a bunch of tiny incisors.

I take another swig of the whiskey before slamming the bottle down on the table. Mr. Mushroom jumps at the sound, so I pat his head and tell him it's okay.

"The last thing I need is a lecture, Drax. I need to know what to do."

Grumbling, he crosses his arms over his short-sleeve hoodie, leans back into my bacteria-infested couch, and breathes out through his slits for nostrils. "Did he see you morph?"

I shake my head. "Don't think so. I broke through the window before pulling my wings out."

He pets his scaly, hairless head. Shrugging, he looks up at me as if the answer is obvious.

"What?" I ask.

His eyelids go flat. "What do you mean, what? The guy knows what you look like. He can identify you at the time and place of the murder. I don't understand why you didn't deal with the situation—"

"I don't know, okay? To be honest, I don't remember much after that Dragon's Tear."

He gives me the look he always gives me when booze gets me into trouble, which has been happening quite often as of late. It's an unimpressed look that translates to, *When are you going to deal with your issues?*

"Maybe next time don't drink a vampire liquor."

I flick my wrist at him. "I'm sure it's no big deal. If I get taken in for questioning, I can easily say I don't remember anything because we were all fucked up on drugs."

"You jumped out the window, Alex. You don't think that'll look suspicious? Look... I know you swore not the kill innocent feebles after—" but he stops himself, knowing full well that if he wants to stay on my good side, he won't talk about what happened.

I make my eyelids go flat. "What do you want me to do? Track him down and make him disappear?"

He shrugs. "You could threaten him. Scare the shit out of him."

Throwing my head back, I let out an irritated grumble. "Whatever. I guess I could just kill him. No one associated with Adam is innocent." I know it's the booze talking, but I don't care. "So, yeah... Maybe I'll kill him to be safe. Later, though. I'm tired."

He points at the half-empty bottle of whiskey. "You aren't tired, you're drunk. Quit your whining, stop drinking, and go kill the bastard."

He's right. I am drunk, and apparently, pretty fucking argumentative when drunk off Dragon's Tear. Thanks to my good fortune, I don't get hangovers, so it isn't hard to maintain a constant state of oblivion. I let out another roar under my breath, chug back another mouthful of the mouthwatering whiskey before Drax can protest, and slam the bottle back on the table.

I get that Drax hates to see me like this, but I'm a grown-ass woman. If I want to drink to take the edge off, that's my prerogative.

Mr. Mushroom jumps again, but this time, I shoo him off my lap. "Sorry, cutie-patootie-little-munchkin-baby. Mommy's gotta go kill someone."

"You're a fuckin' weirdo," Drax says, reaching for the bottle.

Shrugging, I slip my leather boots on, pluck my leather jacket off the back of the couch, and slip my arms through its sleeves. I glance at Drax before leaving my apartment, wanting to tell him, *Thanks for your help, Drax. You're always here for me when I'm at my lowest. Honestly, I think of you as a brother and I love you.* But what comes out instead is, "Takes one to know one, asshole."

Chapter 5

How am I supposed to find some random dude I've seen once and while intoxicated at that? The city's up to a million in population, and there are tons of guys who look like the one I saw—dark features, short black hair, and tattoos running down his neck.

With a sigh, I remind myself that this is what I do for a living. Maybe Drax was right—I should have laid off the Dragon's Tear. Why can't I shake this off? I blink hard, wishing my horrendous memories away. What I wouldn't do to go back in time...

Focus, Alexis.

Closing my eyes, I think back to last night and replay the scenario in my head. Those tattoos... They weren't only on his neck; they also ran down his arms and over his knuckles. I need to remember specifics. I squint harder behind my aviator sunglasses, trying to get a closer look at the image building in my mind.

Dollar symbols.

Okay.

What about the neck? I alter my perspective and try to zoom into his neck as if looking at a computer screen. For someone who drinks as much as I do, my visual memory's pretty damn good. Slowly, it comes back to me. A green dragon with a clock in its mouth. That's a great start. Now, what other details were there?

Focus, Alexis, focus.

Out of nowhere, something hard hits me on the shoulder and my sunglasses make an escape attempt, almost falling right off my face.

"Watch where you're walkin', lady!" a man shouts in my ear as he passes by.

Fucking prick.

I'm about to shout back, "You watch where you're walking, jackass!"

But then I realize I was the one walking with my eyes almost closed. I can be a coldhearted bitch, but I'm not an irrational one—I know when I'm in the wrong, and I refuse to become like one of those road-raging fucktards who flip you off when you honk at them despite *clearly* being in the wrong. San Halos has enough of those already. So instead of biting this guy's head off, I bite my tongue and keep walking down Relik Street, one of the busiest streets in downtown San Halos. It also happens to be one of the most dangerous ones, especially at night.

Maybe that's why I like it so much.

I've spent hours sitting on street benches and

staring at that neon-green street sign.

Relik Street.

Did the city do that on purpose? Did they somehow plan for more than 80 percent of the city's criminal activity to take place here? In the depths of my twisted imagination, a round-shaped man wrapped in a suit too tight for his body sealed the deal. From his tight pocket, he pulled out an overpriced brand-name pen, scowled, and signed the paper as if finalizing a billion-dollar deal. Then, with an unfittingly feminine and throaty voice, he shouted to the rest of his sheep council, "The police will always know where to look! Relik says Killer backward. It's brilliant. Brilliant, I tell you."

I suck in a deep breath through my nose, taking in every scent Relik Street has to offer.

Did I mention I have a keen sense of smell? It proves to be both beneficial and highly disadvantageous at times. For example, I once screwed a guy who was coming back from a long day at work and two hours at the gym. Don't get me wrong... some ladies might be into that, but imagine the smell of sour balls, three-month-old fish, and fresh dog urine thrown into a mix and spread inside your nostrils every few seconds.

Yeah, my senses are *that* heightened.

At the moment, I smell over a thousand distinct smells. Like a dog—I'm more of a fierce tigress, but for this example, I'll allow a dog comparison—I'm able to focus on one specific smell.

And that guy had a smell. I remember it now.

It isn't something I can place or describe. Everyone has scents unique to them. Some are sweet, others spicy, and some downright nauseating. Feebles have a certain smell, too, and that guy was undeniably a feeble.

His scent was a mixture of tangy and spicy, which is like describing a dish cooked by a world-renowned chef as simply, *Yummy*. There's so much more to it, but it's difficult to explain. What I do know is that I'll be filtering through thousands of smells for the next few hours, if not days, trying to track the bastard down.

I'm about to continue marching down Relik Street when I spot a woman stepping out of a Stardust Coffee Shop grasping a massive latte with both hands.

God, what I'd do for a coffee right now. But I remember: I'm not poor. At least not for the next few weeks. I've got plenty of cash sitting in my account. Inhaling an abnormal amount of air through flared nostrils, I attract the *what a nut job stare* as I walk past the woman and sniff her coffee. As I whistle a tune, I make my way inside the shop and come back out with a $10 coffee in hand.

Highway robbery is what that is. I suppose after robbing a dead man, I deserve it.

I chug it down and toss the empty cup into the nearest garbage can. I may be a murderer, but I won't stand for littering. With the taste of hot coffee still in my mouth, I cross the street toward one of the twenty cell phone shops on the street.

The store's bell rings as I make my way inside. Behind a counter cluttered with wires, gadgets, and broken switchboards is a dark-skinned man with a bulb for a nose and a huge septum ring that hangs over his mouth. Underneath this are two sharp fangs that come out of his lower jaw and curl over his upper lip.

Great. A Gorton.

His eyes—all three of them—turn my way the moment he sees me enter. He doesn't smile, likely because he can sense that I'm not a feeble like everyone else in his store. What they see when they look at him is a slightly overweight, brown-skinned man with a grumpy scowl on his face. What I see is a greedy demon known for trickery, thieving, and lying.

While there are tons of different variations of Gortons, they're typically all the same—bad.

More often than not, they keep to themselves and avoid social interaction unless it somehow benefits them. They're usually frowning, too, like this guy. But what gives them away is their scent— aged cheese and dandelions.

His large head appears to expand as I move closer. He watches me but doesn't bother welcoming me into his shop.

"Can I help you?" he finally says, his voice monotone.

I pull off my sunglasses and stare at his name tag. "Is that how you greet a customer... Tony?"

He grunts.

Typical Gorton. Dumb and lacking basic social skills. I'm about to ask him for a cell phone when the television above his head catches my attention.

A woman with yellow hair in the shape of a beehive and a purple button-up shirt talks to the camera as if capable of seeing her audience through every television screen in San Halos. The volume's been muted, but it's hard to miss the white text scrolling across the screen.

Adam Shaw Found Dead in Own Home.

Fuck.

I wait for a sketch of me to pop up on-screen, along with bold text that reads, WANTED. But to my surprise, nothing like that appears on the screen, which means the guy who saw me never called the cops. There's only one explanation for that: he isn't a good guy. And what about the woman? Adam's date? There's no mention of her, either. She's probably a suspect, not that it matters. She won't remember anything that happened and will be useful to the investigation.

When the shop's Gorton grunts, I shift my focus to him and clear my throat. "Oh. Um, sorry... I need a cell. Basic."

He stares at me, a look meant to signify, *Look around, there's plenty here.*

"Okay, wise guy," I say. "Give me your best deal

on a burner and I'll be out of your hair."

Without averting his gaze, he reaches under the counter and pulls out a box of old flip phones.

"Nothing like old school," I say, though what I'm thinking is, *Nothing like old technology without GPS.*

No response.

"How much?"

He rolls his eyes toward the stained box. Barely hanging on is a yellow Post-it Note with $50 scribbled in black. I whip out my wallet and dig around for cash—my preferred method of payment—but come out empty-handed. I must have spent the rest of it at the bar the other night. Sighing, I hand him my debit card. Again, not my first choice. I'm not a fan of anything that can be traced.

"No cards," he says, his deep voice making the glass counter vibrate beneath my palms.

"Are you kidding me?"

I make a habit of going to different shops every time I need a new burner phone. If I were to go to the same place all the time, well... people would wonder why I'm going through a dozen phones per year. Most shops are run by arrogant pricks. Then again, almost everyone in San Halos is an arrogant prick.

The Gorton points at the dirty chipped sign hanging by a rusty chain above his head.

CASH ONLY.

So Gorton-like. Also not a fan of traceable

expenses. They are greedy, after all, and they're known for tax evasion. But that isn't my problem. I'm about to snatch one of the phones and tell him to go fuck himself when I spot a camera sitting at the top left-hand corner of the shop. To further discourage me, Gortons are known for being pretty damn strong. Even against my super strength, he'd put up a good fight.

Not that I'd die.

But that's not the point.

"Tell me you guys at least brought an ATM in here."

He shakes his head and I clench my fist against the counter.

I know punching this asshole in the face is tempting, but don't do it, Alexis.

"I need a fucking phone," I say.

He shrugs. "Get cash."

Keeping my mouth shut, I storm out of his shop, opening the door as hard as I can to make a scene. The bells jingle hard and the door's handle smashes into the wall. A young woman with a boy who looks around two years old steps inside. The kid looks up at me like I'm a monster.

He's either fae and can sense what I am, or I'm *that* scary-looking when I'm pissed off.

"Oh, um, sorry," I mumble, brushing past her.

Thanks for ruining my angry exit.

Finding an ATM isn't difficult to do in San Halos. So I get the cash and mumble to myself the entire way back, pissed off by the amount of work this stupid Gorton is making me do. Am I being immature? Maybe. Okay, definitely. Especially for a thousand-year-old succubus. I wasn't always like this, but ever since that awful day... seeing his hollow, lifeless eyes... I haven't been myself. It's as if I've reverted to being a teenager. Every little thing pisses me off and I'm always in the mood to punch someone in the face. I'm sure the alcohol abuse isn't helping, but it's the only thing that numbs the pain. And I need to forget. I can't stand seeing all that blood in my mind... Seeing his angelic face for the last time. Losing everything I cared about.

I swallow hard, fighting back tears.

When I return to the Gorton's cell shop, I walk up to the counter and throw the cash in his face.

His eyes pop wide open, but that's about it. It's frustrating how little emotion these demons express.

"Thanks for nothing," I say, slamming my hand into the box of cell phones.

Two phones immediately go flying upward and across his shop. The rest of them come pouring out of the box when the cardboard splits, but I don't care.

The Gorton's brows come close together. "Hey!"

Staring him in the face, I grab the first cell that hits my hand and slip it into my pocket. He grimaces at me as if expecting me to pick up the loose phones off his counter, but I don't give a shit what he thinks, and after what he put me through, I won't waste another second in here.

I tug at my leather jacket and turn away.

Before exiting, I spin back one last time to flip him the bird.

He looks so furious that I can't help but smile.

Fucking jackass.

"Ow!"

My elbow smashes into something squishy and I hop sideways. In front of me is an old woman with a veiny hand over her left eye. She stumbles to stand upright on Relik Street's interlock sidewalk and winces like she ate a sour gumball.

With difficulty, she bends down and picks up the cane she must have dropped. The moment she stands upright, something in her back snaps and she squeals. But it must not have hurt that much. She glares at me and balls a bony fist.

"Shit, I'm sorry—"

"What's wrong with you?" she shouts. Her voice is so shrill that I pull my face back.

"It was an accident, lady."

Not seeming to care, she scowls even harder, causing her face to bubble with what appears to be a hundred creases and wrinkles. Without warning, she jabs her cane in the air at me and starts shouting a bunch of nonsense.

"I said I'm sorry," I say, my patience thinning.

Around us, people stop walking to watch the scene, which is making things even more awkward.

Obviously, this lady doesn't understand the meaning of an apology, so there's no point in trying to remedy this with words.

Doing my best to ignore her shouting, I try to walk past her, but she slams her cane into the brick wall, blocking my way.

I'm all for respecting my elders, but I apologized for my mistake. This woman's being a bitch.

"Get the fuck out of my way, you old hag."

Inch by inch, she lowers her cane, her eyes disappearing behind wrinkled folds. I'm about to leave when she says, "Slut."

Okay.

Now, Red is building.

Who does she think she is? I clench my teeth, telling myself that slapping an old woman upside the head won't do me any favors, especially when so many people are watching. So instead, I blow air out of my nostrils, ball my fists, and count to three.

And that's when I see it.

She smirks, revealing a small canine tooth and eyes as black as coal.

Now this makes sense. A siren. Why didn't I sense it? Maybe the smell of her old decaying body masked it from me. Sirens hate me. They always have. And not me personally, but succubi in general. The war's been going on for a long time, and it all boils down to one thing: jealousy.

Sirens age. They lose their beauty, which means they lose their powers. I don't age—I'm immortal, and I'll always be beautiful... and maybe a little vain, but with good reason.

I let out a forced laugh through the side of my mouth—a sound meant to signify, *You're such a pathetic waste of my time*—and shove her cane out of my way. She stumbles backward, trying to make it look like I'm the bad guy. A few people gasp, but it doesn't faze me. If only they knew what she really was. Besides, I'm a hot chick and she's an old bitter woman with a hideous look on her face. I think it's safe to say that most fertile people will gravitate toward taking my side.

At long last, the curious crowd scatters.

Slipping my sunglasses back on, I start up my new phone, adjust the basic start-up settings, and send Jamieson a text:

It's me. New number. No jobs until further notice.

CHAPTER 6

My phone beeps over and over again.

Why not?

Are you drunk?

Alexis, you know you're my baby girl.

Jamieson's trying to sweet-talk me, likely under the impression that I'm having a *female* mood swing. The irony is that I don't get periods. I haven't in centuries. I guess succubus fertility has an expiration date, too, but Jamieson doesn't know anything about that. Letting him think I'm being hormonal is my way of getting back at him for acting so high and mighty all the time. Everyone's afraid of a hormonal bitch.

Ignoring his texts, I shove my phone back into my pocket. I have to focus on finding the guy who saw me at Adam's house. After that, I'll get back onto Jamieson's payroll.

I close my eyes, rebuilding the image of him in my mind when his neck tattoo comes into focus again. It's hard to ignore with how unique it is—a dragon with a clock.

Clock Dragon. That's what I'll call him for now.

My phone goes off again, vibrating against my thigh nonstop. If I weren't so focused on getting this job done, I'd let it vibrate longer.

Irritated by the distraction, I pull my phone out and see Jamieson's number scrolling across the screen. He almost never calls. If I don't pick up now, he won't stop hounding me.

Flipping the phone open, I press it to my ear.

"What's up, Jamieson?"

His voice comes out smooth and flirtatious. "Hey, darling, how're you doing?"

"*Darling*? Jamieson, what do you want?"

"Look, Alexis, if I've said anything to offend you—"

I cut him off. "You didn't. Honestly. I have something I need to take care of and it needs my full attention."

The line goes quiet until finally, he says, "Are you sure, love?"

It comes out sounding like a question pulled out of a different conversation. Why is he being so nice? Something's up. It's almost like he's taunting me... trying to get me to sink my teeth into his bait.

Jamieson knows me too well, and his charming voice breaks me. "Okay. What? What's going on? Spit it out," I say.

"Well," he says. "I have something you're going to want to see."

"I told you I'm busy."

He pauses. "Suit yourself, love."

Grinding my teeth, I squeeze the plastic of my phone until something cracks. "I'll be there soon."

He hangs up, and although I can't see him, I'm certain he's got a smug smile on that pretty face of his. I suppose Clock Dragon can wait an hour. I dip my phone back into my pocket and make my way to the subway, past the metal walls that smell like stale urine, and deep into the underground station.

When the train arrives, I hop on the back and plop myself down into one of its plastic chairs. It's uncomfortable and enough to make me wish it were nighttime so that I could fly over to Jamieson. I don't make a habit of flying around in the sky, but I have done it on several occasions.

Okay, on many occasions. If anyone found out, they'd report me. Every shadow dweller knows that our number one priority is to ensure we don't expose ourselves to feebles.

If someone breaks this rule, they have to explain themselves to the vampires, and everyone knows that vampires aren't forgiving. While the Council of Elders might technically be the ones in charge, everyone knows that vampires run the show. Why? Because they've been around for as long as anyone can remember and they reproduce like fucking rabbits. That makes them the mafia of the Underworld. If you cross one, you cross them all, and if you reveal yourself to a feeble, you're basically crossing them because you're fucking with their source of food.

Silent, I sit with arms crossed, while in front of me, three young guys sit across an entire row of seats, throwing jabs at each other.

Why didn't I bring my baseball cap? I quiet my breath, hoping I'll go unnoticed. The one downside to being a succubus is that the moment a man or woman gets a good look at me, they *want* to talk to me. They want more than that, but they start it off with a conversation.

Sometimes I just want to be left the fuck alone.

Through the window behind the three guys, I glimpse my reflection: black hair pulled back into a high ponytail, piercing blue eyes, high cheekbones that could easily have me mistaken for a vampire, and plush pink lips.

To any feeble, I'm considered beautiful.

Hell, I'm fucking hot. The first week after my transformation, I spent days staring at myself in the mirror, wishing I could duplicate my new body and fuck myself for weeks.

"Hey," comes a rugged voice.

Without turning my head, I look over at the guy in the middle. Clearly, he's the one with the most testosterone and the most confidence. He elevates his square jaw and stares at me hungrily.

Ignoring him, I shift my position and lean my head against the window behind me.

He seems to enjoy that I want nothing to do with him... most guys do. It's the chase they want.

Others simply like it when a chick's a bitch.

"Where's your boyfriend?" He elbows his buddies and lets out an obnoxious laugh. "I mean... He shouldn't let you travel all by yourself in this dangerous city."

I cock an eyebrow. "Why's that, Peppermint?"

He doesn't seem to find this funny, but his red-and-green-striped shirt was begging to be insulted. Besides, I want him to feel small. I fucking hate it when men insinuate that women shouldn't be left unescorted by a male. "Think I can't handle myself?"

He nudges his buddies again. They laugh but avoid eye contact with me. It's obvious Peppermint is in charge. His friends are either more respectful than he is, or they can sense that I'm not the kind of woman to put up with bullshit like this.

Peppermint licks his lips. His eyes crinkle with amusement and he lowers his gaze to my chest. "Oh, I bet you can handle yourself."

How late would I be for my meeting with Jamieson if I took care of this little shithead?

"Did your mother teach you to talk like that?" I ask.

He doesn't say anything. Instead, he stares at me with such intensity it's obvious he's picturing dirty things. He searches my chest, my hips, and then my lips.

Guys like him can be handled in one of two ways.

1) I could beat the shit out of him until he cries for his mom.

2) I could have fun and feed.

While they're both satisfying options, the latter is the one option in which I get to feed. And with how angry I've been lately, a good meal is what I need.

Leaning forward, I squeeze my arms around my breasts to make them pop out. He follows my bait, almost salivating. Beside him, his friends laugh uncomfortably and the one nearest to him punches him in the shoulder.

"Dude, leave her alone."

It's too late. He's already pissed me off, so now, it's time for my Lure.

It takes a few seconds for his face to change completely. He stiffens his posture, loosens his jaw, and watches me as if I were Cleopatra risen from the dead.

"Fuck... You're... You're gorgeous," he says.

"And you're a bad boy," I say, biting my lower lip. "Whaddaya say we get out of here?"

Although I'm directing my Lure onto Peppermint, his buddies are getting some of it, too. A few jumbled words come out of their mouths, but it doesn't make much sense.

The moment the subway comes to a stop, I grab Peppermint's hand and step out into the subway station. We're right underneath Second Street, which is where I'm headed to find Jamieson, anyways.

This won't take long.

As I lead him to the men's washroom, my heels clacking against the cement floor, his friends follow us like puppets on strings.

"You two," I say, pointing a finger at them. "Wait here."

They nod like robots and stand in the middle of the subway, looking like total morons. I know what they're thinking: *If we sit here like good little boys, we'll get our turn, too.*

They can dream.

While feeding off all three at once would be intense, I'm not up to doing it with feebles. It takes a lot of concentration not to kill one, let alone three.

Peppermint doesn't say a word as I lead him toward the men's washroom. He already has a boner, and he's breathing so loudly I wonder if I'll even get to have my way with him before he explodes in his pants.

The moment I bust open the washroom door, a few guys pull their parts inside their pants and bend forward to cover themselves.

"Whoa, lady."

"Yo, man."

"Get out," I say coldly.

They zip their flies and run out of the bathroom, heads turning toward me as they exit. The moment they're out, I lock the door, grab the man by the face and push him up against the tiled wall, right beside one of the urinals.

I lick his neck, then nibble his ear and whisper, "What's your name, bad boy?"

"T-T-Tommy," he stammers.

"Tommy," I breathe, grabbing him under the belt.

A deep moan exits his mouth, and he closes his eyes. "Holy shit..."

Giving him an expressionless stare, I unzip his jeans and reach inside.

He wants this so bad it could kill him.

But he isn't getting anything yet. I find the more I tease my toy, the more satisfying my meal is—for me and for my prey.

I watch him squirm against the tile wall as I slowly unzip the front of my jeans. Although I don't show it, I'm dying to have another meal. When I get hungry—and now I'm fucking starving—a primal instinct takes over, making me want sex more than anything in the world.

His face swells with excitement, and he looks like he's about to stroke out. I sway my hips from side to side, allowing my jeans and panties to drift down my legs. They don't even have the time to reach my ankles. With popping jaw muscles and a wild look in his eyes, he lunges at me and grabs me by my waist.

If I weren't so hungry, I'd put him in his place, but the truth is, my Lure makes me want this as badly as he does. Together, we stumble across the bathroom until my bare ass hits the wall behind me.

He can't wait.

He doesn't.

Gripping my throat as tightly as he can—which doesn't feel like much coming from a feeble—he takes me. The feeling is out of this world... a euphoria only succubi understand.

With my chin resting on his shoulder, I glance up at the mirror across the room. Cupping a hand at the back of his neck, I smile up at my own reflection as my black hair and blue eyes turn white.

It's happening.

Slowly, my horns pierce through, sticking straight up into the air.

"Don't stop," I say.

His rapid breath beats against my neck as he slams me into the wall.

He does as he's been told, his face glistening and turning a deeper shade of red.

Suddenly, euphoria explodes within me.

I grab him by the face, kissing him hard.

He stumbles backward and falls to the floor, bringing me down with him. Still straddling his waist, I suck on his mouth, pulling out his succulent life force.

At first, I taste my prize, but as the energy revitalizes me, I suck harder and harder, wanting to consume him in full. The only problem is... if I don't stop in time, I'll kill him. And although part of me wants to hurt him for being such a pig earlier, he's still a feeble, and I'd be murdering an innocent man in cold blood.

Digging my claws into the tiled floor, I push myself off and growl at the ceiling in frustration. Under me, he lies still, his glazed eyes fixated on me as if I were his lifelong fantasy come to life... which I probably am.

I rip my claws out of the tiles and climb off. But all of a sudden, he groans—the sound a stark contrast to the pleasured groans from earlier—and clutches at his chest.

Would you look at that... karma. The prick's having a heart attack.

I smile down at him, wanting nothing more than to press the heel of my boot into his aching chest. Instead, I run my fingers through my hair, put my pants back on, fix my top, and wink down at him. "Thanks for the meal, Tommy."

He's in too much pain to respond. He grimaces up at me, then grabs at the air, trying desperately to get me to help him.

As if I'd help a douchebag like him.

That's my inner rage talking—many years of built-up anger. The truth is, he's only a feeble, and I'm not *that* cold-hearted.

Rolling my eyes, I move toward the bathroom's exit and force my smile off my face. If there's one thing I'm good at aside from sex, it's acting.

I unlock the door, swing it open, and run out into the crowd. "Help, someone! He's having a heart attack!"

CHAPTER 7

By the time the police and paramedic lights come flashing down Second Street, I'm walking with my head held high, my aviator sunglasses on, and a smug smile on my face.

God, I feel refreshed.

Nothing like an afternoon meal to pump me up.

I hop up the stairs of Jamieson's Palace, one of the fanciest hotels in the city. It's also the hotel Jamieson owns. The moment I walk inside, Miguel, the hotel's youngest concierge, beams at me as I make my way to the elevators. They're made entirely of glass, so when I turn around, I catch him checking out my ass.

He looks away, his cheeks growing pink, and he goes off to help an old lady bring her luggage inside.

"Alexis," Jamieson says the moment I enter his office.

He waves to his security guards, signaling them to leave the room, then stands and stretches his arms out. "So lovely to see you."

Today, he's clad in a blue suit with shiny brown

shoes that look like they've been scrubbed about a hundred times by house elves. Not only does Jamieson have an attractive British accent, but he's also charming in every sense of the word. It's no wonder all the ladies want him.

All the ladies but me.

He offers a slight bow, his salt and pepper hair pointing my way, and rubs the stubble on his face. "Are you all right?"

I plop myself down into the oversized leather chair across from his deck and kick my feet up. "I'm good. What's up?"

He clears his throat. "I believe this conversation may be better entertained in my private room."

I nod, allowing my sunglasses to slide down my nose. "Private room? Jamieson, I already told you. You aren't my type."

He smiles, revealing overly white and perfectly aligned teeth. "Come."

"Buy me dinner first," I say.

Shaking his head, he leads me to the back of his office and through a thick, mahogany door. The space looks more like a lounge room. A red leather sofa sits invitingly against a black wall, reminding me of my therapist's office, and in front of it is an oval glass coffee table. At the other end of the room stands a humongous fridge and a few feet away from it, a gigantic television.

Is this where he lets loose?

"I've never brought you here," he says, "but

believe me... you want to see this."

I'm about to say, *No shit... If you had, I'd come over more often*, but I follow quietly.

Where the hell is he taking me? He reaches behind his television and pulls back on something—assumedly a lever. Out of nowhere, part of the wall next to his fridge sinks in and disappears altogether, revealing an opening the size of a doorframe.

He smirks back at me. "Come."

I'm too intrigued to bother retorting with a sexual joke.

The moment we step inside, bright lights flash overhead, illuminating the entire room. It's filled with computer monitors, machine guns, and a rack of weapons.

My jaw hangs loose as I gaze around. "Is this where you work?"

He nods.

I walk up to the weapons rack and brush my fingers along the crossbows, the axes, and a brown-handled sword that looks sharp enough to cut someone without even touching them.

"Why are you only showing me this now?" I ask.

While I'm thrilled to be seeing such a cool place, I'm a little annoyed that he didn't show me sooner. I could have used some of these weapons.

"How long have we known each other, Alexis?"

I shrug. "Couple years."

"You've completed sixty-two jobs for me," he

says.

"Sixty-three," I correct him, and he smiles.

"What if I told you I had the most challenging job yet?"

All right, now I'm curious.

He reaches for a remote and turns the monitors on. Images of a woman's silhouette appear on each one, all from various angles and seemingly different eras. It's odd—not a single image shows her face. Some are black and white, others sketches, and some 3D creations. In one image, she's clad in attire from the late 1920s, and in another, she's sporting a pantsuit.

"Who is she?" I ask.

"Someone who is getting in my way," Jamieson says.

While Jamieson portrays himself as a highly educated and peaceful English man, he's beyond dangerous. He's nice to me, but that's because I work for him. The truth is, I wouldn't want to cross him, and that's saying a lot being that he's a feeble.

He owns over half the city in real estate and has made it clear that if anyone stands in his way, he'll cut them down. He's corrupt in more ways than I can count, but I choose not to ask questions. All I care about is getting paid.

"So you want me to take her out?" I ask. "Why's she so interesting? Is she important or something?"

"Don't worry about the details." He stares at the images. In a flash, his charming smile transforms into a spiteful grimace. Then, he tugs at the collar of his expensive overcoat and says, "Five million dollars."

My jaw drops.

"Five million—"

"Five million," he confirms.

"What's the catch?" I ask.

"No catch—only risk. Veerka Vanmorte. She's incredibly dangerous." He throws his chin out toward the rack of weapons. "You'll be needing some of those."

Dangerous? How dangerous could this woman possibly be? Some of the images look over a century old, and in each picture, she looks the same. The woman doesn't age, which means she's likely a vampire. She could be fae, but if Jamieson wants her dead, it means she's implicated in some shady shit... which, let's face it, most vampires are.

And if that's the case, so what? I've killed hundreds of vampires. That still doesn't explain why she's such a threat.

Unless...

"Before you ask... This job is highly classified, but I'm told it's been shared exclusively over the last few weeks."

"So others have already tried and failed," I say, matter-of-factly.

Jamieson nods.

That explains why the price tag is so high. No one's been able to kill her. How come? Does she have protection? Is she some super ancient vampire with incredible power? I know Jamieson won't talk about the whole vampire thing, so I don't bring it up.

"What makes you think I'll succeed?" I ask.

"You're the best I've ever had."

Although flattered by his compliment, I can't help but wonder why he didn't come to me first. Why let others go after her if I'm the best he has? Over the last few months, Jamieson's made it quite clear that I've earned his top position, meaning I get offered jobs before anyone else does. If I'm his second choice on this one, it means something's up.

"What aren't you telling me?"

Clenching his jaw, he sighs. "She's a *vampire*." He almost snarls the last word.

I'm shocked to hear that word come out of his mouth. Jamieson doesn't talk about demons or vampires. He likes to pretend they don't exist. He knows all about the magical world, and he hates it. He also hates that vampires run the Underworld. It's a power thing. I'm willing to bet that if he had the chance, he'd take them out so he could rule over all of San Halos.

So is that what he means when he says this woman is getting in his way? It must be political, which means he has to tread carefully. After all, he can't have his name on this kill if he wants to keep running shit. He might not like vampires, but he needs to keep the peace with them, which means he needs me to do his dirty work.

"I didn't want to implicate you in this, Alexis, but you're my only hope. Take her out, and the five million dollars is yours." He crosses his arms over his chest with a twinkle in his eyes. He knows I love a challenge as much as I love money. That being said, I'm insulted that he'd send me out on a suicide mission, especially since he thinks I'm a feeble. He either doesn't give a shit about my life or he does have that much faith in me. It's hard to believe either of those options. Maybe he's so blinded by his hatred for this woman that he can't see past his own nose.

When I don't answer, he tilts his head. "What do you say, Alexis? I know you can do this."

I push my tongue against the inside of my cheek, mulling everything over. Five million dollars is life-changing, but so is getting involved with vampires... and I would know. Been there, done that. This isn't about not being able to; it's about not being dumb enough to do it. At the end of the day, I've fought long and hard to build a life for myself here in San Halos without upsetting the Vampire Mafia. If I succeed in doing this and I get caught, vampires won't stop hunting me down until I'm dead—permanently. I could flee to Mexico and it wouldn't matter. Vampires communicate all around the world, and if this woman is as important as Jamieson is making her out to be—which, obviously, she is if she has a five-million-dollar bounty on her head—killing her is a death sentence.

Now biting the inside of my cheek, I shake my head. "Sorry, James. Not this time."

He parts his lips, clearly wanting to convince me otherwise, but I turn around before he can use his British accent against me. Right before exiting his secret room, I reach for leather cuffs hanging on the wall and strap them on. With a flick of my wrists, two sharp six-inch blades come tearing out of secret compartments and lock into place.

"Holy shit, that's cool," I say.

Jamieson is likely too stunned by my rejection of the job to say anything.

I'm about to step out when I glimpse a slick black crossbow that caught my eye earlier. It's made of coated metal, an elastic that looks indestructible, and a large scope at the top.

I can sense Jamieson watching me, so I hesitate.

Ah, fuck it. I think after everything I've done for this man, I deserve a bonus.

I snatch it off the wall, sending mounting equipment flying across the room. Then, I grab the black leather quiver sitting next to it, filled with a dozen silver bullet arrows.

"What do you think you're doing?" he blurts out at last. "That's a five-thousand-dollar—"

So much for my bonus.

Without looking back, I wave the crossbow over my head. "You can dock this off my next pay."

CHAPTER 8

Mr. Mushroom bolts off Drax's lap and heads straight for me, his little nails ticking against my parquet flooring.

I bend down and am greeted by slimy kisses. "Hey, buddy."

"We were cuddling," Drax says dryly, his expression flat.

"Well, excuse me," I say. "What're you still doing here, anyway? Don't you work today?"

Drax shakes his thick horned head. "Jake canceled my shift."

"Jake as in the manager?"

He nods.

I've heard about Jake countless times. He's the manager of TruMart and tends to treat his employees like garbage. Well, most of them. He's overly nice to the young, pretty girls. Guys, not so much. And especially not to Drax.

Feebles see Drax as a tall guy with messy brown hair, torn jeans, plain T-shirts, and Converse. Jake, more importantly, views Drax as a punk who can't quite seem to find his path in life and treats him accordingly. Or, more bluntly... he thinks of him as a stoner with no ambition in life. I'd be lying if I said it wasn't entirely true. While I love Drax and consider him family, he needs to get his shit together. Ever since he got rejected by his parents after trying to reach out again, he's spiraled down a dark path.

That was eight years ago. He was nineteen.

All right, maybe I shouldn't judge. We're on the same path, and I've been around for over a thousand years. I guess that makes *me* the one who needs to get my shit together.

I pull off my sunglasses and toss them on top of a pile of jackets I stole last week. "I'm sorry Jake's being such a dick. I can kill him if you want."

That's my way of saying, *I'm sorry about this, buddy. I'm here if you need to talk.*

Drax smiles. He knows I'm only joking. "Thanks, Alex. Do you mind if I crash here for a while?"

Planting my hands on my hips, I tilt my head. "You mean you don't already live here?"

This time, he laughs. Drax has an apartment... somewhere. He's never there. Most of the time, he's here. So the running joke is that he's my roommate, but he doesn't pay me any rent.

"Stay as long as you need," I say. "You know you're always welcome here."

The words feel mushy coming out of my mouth, so I clear my throat, head to the fridge, and pull out a beer. Cracking it open, I jerk my chin out at him. "Want one?"

"It's ten in the morning."

I take a gulp. "What's your point?"

When he doesn't answer, I make my way back into the living room and plop down across from him. "Do you know who Veerka Vanmorte is?"

Mr. Mushroom licks the condensation off my beer, and Drax stares at us like we're some disgusting couple showing too much affection in public.

"Sounds like a vampire," he says matter-of-factly.

"She is." I take another sip. "But I'm trying to figure out who she is and why she's so important."

He plays with one of his horns—a habit of his when he's thinking hard. "I don't know, Alex. I haven't exactly been social these last few years. You know I'm not involved with anyone from the Underworld aside from you."

Sighing, I pat Mr. Mushroom on the head.

"Why are you asking me?" he says.

Drax knows what I do for a living. Typically, I don't go into the gritty details with him. It's more of a thing we don't talk about unless I desperately need his help, like with my hit on Adam Shaw. We treat my profession as if I were a spy for the federal government. It isn't talked about unless absolutely necessary.

"It's a job I rejected," I admit.

"Because she's a vampire," Drax says.

I nod. While Jamieson's never sent me on a hunt after a vampire before, I've always told Drax that if he did, I'd reject the job. Drax knows how I feel about vampires, especially after what they did. This is the first time I've said no to Jamieson, so it isn't hard for Drax to put two and two together.

"What was the payout?" he asks.

Again, this is something I've only talked to Drax about twice. Once, when I got excited about my ten-grand job with Jamieson, and again when I was offered fifty grand a few days ago to take out Adam.

"Five million," I say.

Drax's jaw drops and Mr. Mushroom barks in my face as if trying to tell me to take the job.

"Holy fuck, Alex. You need to take it."

Glaring at him, I tighten my grip around my beer bottle's neck and it cracks. "You aren't on my life insurance policy, Drax. So I don't know why you're encouraging a suicide mission."

He rolls his eyes. "Please. You can't afford life insurance with how you keep throwing your money away. Besides, this isn't about me. Think about how much your life could change, Alex. You could get yourself a nice place"—he gestures upward, pointing out all the cobwebs and busted ceiling tiles overhead—"and not have to worry about bills for a while." He leans back into the sofa, rests both arms on the back cushions, and gives me a sly smile that makes it impossible for me to be angry with him. "And I could quit my job and move in with you."

I tear a couch cushion right out from underneath Mr. Mushroom's butt and throw it at Drax's face. He catches it with his brown clawed fingers and laughs—a rumbly sound I don't hear too often.

"There's a reason she's worth that much," I say.

With one claw, he scratches his chin. "Yeah, guess you're right. Well, listen, before you say no to the job—"

"I already said no. Why are you trying to push me into this? You know damn well my Lure doesn't always work on vampires. It's a huge risk. And even if I manage to kill her, can you imagine the repercussions? I'll have a huge price on my head."

I want to add, "Besides, feeding off a vampire is like eating air," but I don't, because this debate isn't about how much my kill will satisfy me sexually. It's about the money.

He waves a hand in front of his face as if trying to erase everything that came out of his mouth. "Sorry... Look. Forget what I said. But, if you change your mind, I do know a guy—"

My eyes start to narrow.

Drax and I both know why I refuse to go after vampires. He should know better than to push me.

"You came to me, Alex. You were curious. So if you want your questions answered, I know a guy. That's all I'm saying. But I totally understand why you wouldn't want—"

"A guy who will know who she is?" I ask.

"He knows everything. He gets paid to share information. That's what he does. I haven't talked to him in years, but I know where he is."

I finish my beer and place the cracked bottle on the coffee table alongside another dozen empties and my Dragon's Tear whiskey. My gaze lingers on the whiskey longer than intended before Drax says, "Alex!"

"Relax," I say. "I wasn't going to have any."

Especially not after it turned me into a raging bitch who almost knocked out an old lady.

With a swing of my body, I get up and Mr. Mushroom starts scratching at my legs.

"He has to pee," Drax says.

"Can you let him out?" I reach into a pile of clothes behind the couch and pull out a black baseball cap. From it, I pluck off a piece of dry apple and throw it into Mr. Mushroom's mouth.

What the hell have I become? I used to pay people to do my laundry.

"Consider pee duty your new job," I say. "It'll count as your rent paid to stay here."

"Where are you going?" he asks.

I put my hat on, slide my arms into my leather jacket's sleeves, slip on my boots, and blow Mr. Mushroom a kiss.

"To finish a job."

CHAPTER 9

Police cruisers sit on the side of the road, some with their bright blue and red lights flashing, others without. A few black SUVs are also present, and it's hard to tell whether they belong to the police or someone else.

Yellow crime scene tape borders Adam Shaw's property. It starts at his front iron gates, runs along his perfectly trimmed cedar hedges, and leads all the way to the back of the house. How much tape did they put? The guy's property is huge. Talk about a waste of taxpayer dollars.

I flew over his backyard last night—the bastard owns (well, owned) a tennis court, a basketball court, an in-ground swimming pool the size of a house, and too many other things to list without getting pissed off about it.

Keeping my head low under the shade of my hat, I join the crowd that's formed behind a metal barrier. People bicker, some pointing fingers, while others play aggressively on their phones. What do they think they'll find? Some Instagram photo that somehow becomes evidence?

Please. I took his phone and wiped all of his accounts.

Sweeping through the crowd of curious bystanders, I poke my head over their shoulders, trying to catch a conversation worth listening to.

"Do you know what happened?" a young man asks.

The middle-aged woman standing beside him places a hand over her mouth and shakes her head somberly. "The police aren't revealing anything."

"Was he murdered?"

"I heard something about a suicide."

"Nah, I doubt that. The guy was living the dream. I bet someone was hired to kill him."

I scoff so loudly that several heads turn my way. Quickly, I lower my baseball cap until it touches the top of my sunglasses and walk away from the group of gossipers.

There are too many smells here, making it close to impossible to track Clock Dragon's scent. But it has to be here somewhere. It hasn't even been twenty-four hours yet, so I'm bound to find something. All I need is a whiff, and I should be able to trace it back to him.

One woman chewing gum plants a hand over her belly—a belly so large it looks like she ate a donkey. She smacks her lips, sucking her saliva, and swallows whatever taste remains in her piece of gum.

Her half-toothed mouth opens wide. "Ain't make no sense. He was fine yesterday. Get those damn cops over here. You! Yeah, you! Y'all need to tell us what the hell's goin' on here."

America's finest.

Her hot breath floats through the air and slips up my nose, causing bile to creep up my throat.

She should request a refund on that gum.

Holding my breath, I turn away until it's safe to breathe again.

Finally, I catch something. The smell is faint... so faint it's barely there at all. But it is there. It's him—the Clock Dragon guy. Where is that son of a bitch? He didn't stay long last night. Otherwise, I'd have a better scent. I start twirling in circles, following my nose like a brain-damaged hound.

People must think I'm drunk.

Nothing new there.

At last, I catch a trail and start following my nose. It leads me away from the crime scene, down Apple Hill Road, and across another dozen million-dollar homes. It still isn't overly strong, which means he isn't anywhere near here.

So I walk, and walk, and walk... wishing I'd brought a bottle of tequila with me. The trail leads me back into the city and toward a neighborhood I tend to avoid—Estreenos. By the time I get there, the sun's already starting to set.

How long have I been walking? It's not like my feet get sore enough to provide any sort of measure; I've been alive far too long for that.

Oh God. Is this where he lives? As I enter the neighborhood, little Latino kids carrying basketballs and rocks look at me like I've lost my way. Keeping my head down, I continue to follow the trail. It leads me to a shoddy old house with a busted window, crisp yellow grass, pieces of garbage across the lawn, a short chain-link fence, and a beaten Honda Civic without tires.

On the front concrete steps, a young Latino boy rests his face in his palms. He looks up at me as I continue down the road, careful not to draw too much attention to myself.

No question, the smell is coming from that house.

So who's the kid?

"Pedro!" comes an angry woman's voice.

The kid's eyes bulge, but he doesn't move.

Then, out through the screen door comes a young Latina woman with hoop earrings, too-long pink fingernails, a very pregnant belly, and tattoos running down her left arm. She pulls her wavy chocolate-brown hair over one shoulder, chews a piece of gum with her mouth wide open, and grabs at her curvy waist.

As she chews, she yells at the boy in Spanish, and although I can't make out what she's saying, it's obvious she's telling him to get back inside. When he doesn't listen, she grabs him by the arm and pulls him up. As much as I want to barge in there and demand information, I can't do that. She might not know anything. So instead, I make a left turn, cut across someone's tiny yard, and head toward the back of the affordable housing across the street.

If I can't go inside, I'll have to find a spot to hide out until I see the guy. The smell's pretty strong, so he's either inside, or he left not too long ago. Beside the house across from his stands a massive maple tree—the perfect hideout.

I glance around quickly to make sure no one's watching this lunatic climb a tree, then dig my claws into the bark and propel myself into the air. The leaves shake all around me, and if anyone is looking, they must think a couple of cats are fighting on a branch.

I find a good vantage point and straddle one of the largest branches. Having it between my legs isn't exactly comfortable, but it's keeping me in place, and it's also helping me ignore the need to piss badly.

So I lean forward, resting my chest along the branch, and drop my chin onto my palms.

This could take a while.

"Where are you, you son of a bitch?" I whisper to myself.

The sky above darkens to an indigo blue, and the children of the neighborhood scatter throughout the streets, playing with sticks and holding them up like they're guns. A few adults walk along the sidewalks—mostly young men with baggy pants, tattoos on their necks and faces, and bandanas around their black-haired heads.

Everyone knows to stay away from this neighborhood.

Aside from Relik street, it's one of the city's most dangerous places to be at night.

The sound of gunshots in this neighborhood is as common as the sound of lawnmowers in suburbia.

Criminals roam the streets, fighting each other in one of the city's biggest and most recent drug wars. Some of Estreenos's street gangs work for the vampires, supplying both live and packaged blood in exchange for some of the most hardcore drugs available on the streets.

And feebles think the war on drugs is bad... They have no idea how bad it is and how many people are involved.

Estreenos is the kind of place that the municipal government views as toxic but does nothing to fix the root of the problem. Maybe if they brought good schools to the area and worked on fixing the drug trafficking problem, the kids would stand a chance.

As the sun sets, a cool breeze sweeps through the air and kids run back inside their homes. That's when the big fancy drug trafficking cars make their appearances, the overhead streetlights reflecting off their shiny hoods.

One black car with tinted windows and a blue underglow rolls in with loud music blaring from what I can only assume is an expensive aftermarket audio system. It drives slowly as if inspecting the area.

Is that how Clock Dragon's window got busted? Was it a drive-by shooting? Because it looks like that's what these guys are about to do. But instead of pulling out a gun, they suddenly take off with squealing tires.

I'm left disappointed, having wanted to see some action.

A few minutes later, a black, silver-rimmed Escalade rolls in. The music stops when it reaches the front of Clock Dragon's house (or at least what I'm assuming is his house) and out of the passenger doors comes a gang with blue bandanas on their heads and guns in their grips.

When the driver steps out, I clench my fists.

That's him. Clock Dragon. Although his tattoo is hard to see in the dark, there's enough light being cast from above to make it visible.

Apparently, he has an entire crew.

Awesome.

Does he even give a shit that Adam Shaw died? Maybe I'm overreacting. Maybe I did this guy a favor. Adam must have been involved in drugs or something, and maybe he owed one of the gangs some cash.

That's a possibility, right?

Although tempted to climb down and head home, I wait.

Suddenly, a light turns on through the busted kitchen window, and out comes the woman from earlier—the one who yelled at poor little Pedro. She throws her arms around Clock Dragon's neck and kisses him hard.

So they're together... And she's pregnant. That means if I kill the bastard, I'm leaving not only a sad boy without a father but also an unborn child.

Although I can't hear anything they're saying, Clock Dragon waves his arms around animatedly, and his girlfriend, or whoever she is, seems to be getting excited. She covers her mouth and presses her face into his chest.

Good news? Bad news?

He kisses her one last time before turning around, tells his buddies to get back into the SUV, and climbs inside. His tires squeal as he takes off.

Where the hell is he going now?

Father or not, I can't let him get away. He's seen my face, and if he describes me to the cops, I'll have to change my name again and leave the city when I finally found a place I like.

No way.

So I do the one thing I can think of—I blast myself upward and out of the tree, causing several branches to snap. With my wings fully expanded, I propel myself into the sky and follow the gang's Escalade from above.

Chapter 10

Clock Dragon steps out of his Escalade and hands his keys over to some dude at the front of the club. Everyone knows this place—Rova Nightclub. It's San Halos's most exclusive nightclub; it fills up with models, celebrities, and entrepreneurs from all over the states.

They'll never let me inside.

No one gets in unless they're on the list. And that means there's no way I'm sneaking past the two huge bouncers standing at the front.

If Clock Dragon's going in there, it means he's a somebody... It means he has power in this city or he's working for someone who does. Either way, this isn't good.

I glance up at the roof, wondering if maybe I can somehow slip inside from a different entrance. A window? Unlikely. There are guards all around the place, and I highly doubt anyone would leave a rooftop entrance unguarded.

The only way inside is through the front door, and the only way I'm getting in there is if I use my

Lure to convince the bouncers to let me in. The baseball cap on my head feels heavy, as does my leather jacket. Compared to all the hot girls going in there, I'll be mistaken for a homeless chick.

I need a new wardrobe.

Leaning forward on the rooftop, I glance into the dark alleyway, making sure no one's around. When I'm certain no one will report me to the vampires for flying, I lunge off, expand my wings, and land in the alley, my powerful gust causing loose garbage to fly about sporadically.

Alleys are often the best place to land inside the city because no one's around. Well, for the most part. Last year, a homeless guy popped his head out of a dumpster with a half-eaten burger hanging out of his mouth. He pointed a crooked finger at me and started accusing me of being one of Satan's angels.

So I played along and told him that if he told anyone what he saw, I'd send him straight to hell. Although amusing, it was unnecessary—no one will believe him anyway.

Little by little, I step out of the alleyway and into the lights of downtown San Halos, where music blares every time someone opens a door.

"Where are you?" comes a woman's voice. "You said you'd be here, Max. I've been waiting for, like, five minutes and I'm not waiting much longer."

The woman is wearing nine-inch heels, a blue velvet dress so short I can see her butt cheeks, thousands of dollars' worth of gold around her neck, and large hoop earrings so heavy they're causing her ears to droop.

Now *that's* a dress.

And she's all alone.

This is perfect.

"Excuse me," I say, walking up to her.

"Just get over here," she says quickly into her phone. She lowers it and gives me a full up-and-down look that translates to, *Which dumpster did you climb out of?*

She even goes as far as to take a step away from me, which is insulting. I may not be dressed to the nines like she is, but this leather jacket took a lot of work to steal.

"Can I help you?" she asks, her voice nasal.

God. The epitome of a rich, entitled snob.

I almost repeat, "Can I help you?" in an even more nasal voice to mock her, but I bite my tongue. The better part of my brain tells me how immature that would be.

Besides, I need her. So instead of insulting her, I bring out my friendly, extra chipper voice and say, "Oh, yeah, I'm so sorry to bother you—"

And then I trip over my feet on purpose and throw my hat off my head. It lands by her feet, right where I want it to.

"Oh shit," I say. "Sorry about that."

She takes another step back, her hands curled up next to her breasts as if I vomited on the sideway.

"What's your problem?" she says.

Instead of answering, I bend down, grab my hat, then gently wrap my fingers around one of her ankles, admiring her leather-strapped heel. "Wow. These are gorgeous."

I can activate my Lure from a close distance, but it works faster with touch.

This time, she doesn't pull away.

"Like, really stunning," I add, now gliding a gentle finger along the leather, around her ankle, up her calf, and close to her inner thigh. She instinctively parts her legs, her heel scratching the cold asphalt.

"I-I... Um... Thank you."

Slowly, I rise back up, gliding the tip of my finger across her soft, shaven thigh and up the side of her hip. We stand face-to-face, and I smirk, focusing my gaze on her lips.

"They suit you," I say.

She gasps, but it's obvious she's too excited to say anything.

Good. She'd better be excited. I want her to beg me for it.

I reach for her shoulder. "You look tense."

The moment I squeeze, she closes her eyes and her skin bubbles with thousands of little goose bumps.

"You need to relax," I say, massaging her muscles.

She nods, her head rocking back and forth.

My Lure is working full force.

Saying nothing, I grab her hand and lead her into the darkness of the alleyway. She doesn't hesitate—she's so exhilarated that she drops her purse along with her cell phone and follows me, her heels ticking fast and hard against the asphalt.

The moment we disappear into the darkness, I turn around, wrap my fingers in her hair, and push her backward until her back goes flat against the brick wall. She winces as if it's hurting her, but in reality, she's loving it. The corner of her mouth pulls up with excitement, and her eyelids flutter.

"You like that?" I say, wanting nothing more than to give her a taste of heaven. I let go of her hair and instead reach for her throat. Her breath quickens, as does her heartbeat against my palm, and she licks her lips.

You want this, don't you? I say in my mind.

Although she can't hear me, she nods and grabs my wrist as a way of telling me to squeeze tighter. Next, her frightened, honey-brown eyes meet mine, and her desire becomes obvious to me. Fear turns her on.

I can work with that.

I've fed off my share of submissive women before, but this one's different—she craves aggression so much I have to consciously stop myself from crushing her throat. With my Lure in full force, I need to be careful.

Breathing out through clenched teeth, I tighten my grip around her jugular—not too tight, but tight enough that she struggles to breathe.

"Just take me," she says, her voice constricted.

I pull her dress up hard and give her exactly what she wants. With eyes rolled back, she moans and bites her bottom lip, then reaches for the brick above her head and claws at it.

She digs her fingernails into my arm. Blood trickles down my skin, which is always a good sign. She's no longer thinking with her mind. A raw, primal urge has taken over, and she wants me more than she wants to breathe.

Right now, I want the same thing.

Goose bumps erupt all over my body as the high kicks in. I lick her neck, her shoulder, and run the tips of my pointed teeth across her chin.

After I finish, she bites her lower lip and stares into me as if I've injected her with heroin. And while I'd love to go at it again, it's something else that I want. With my thumb, I pull her plush lip down and kiss her hard. My favorite purple mist comes spilling out through the corners of our mouths as I enjoy my euphoric meal.

It energizes me instantly, making me want to suck harder. I can feel my hair lighten to a white and my eye color starts to change. If I don't stop now, I'll kill her.

It takes everything in me to stop—she tastes so fucking good I could suck her dry.

Clock Dragon.

Clock Dragon.

I have a mission.

Punching a hole through the brick wall behind her, I pull away. She lets out a quivering breath before her knees buckle. I catch her midfall, admiring the dazed look on her face, and slowly position her limp body atop the alleyway's cobblestones.

When she wakes up—and that's a big *when*—she'll have no recollection of what happened.

With any luck, her loser boyfriend will find her before some homeless pervert does.

Ah, hell. I'll send someone her way before I go after Clock Dragon.

I look around to make sure I don't have an audience, then tear off my jacket, my shirt, and my pants until I'm left standing in my bra and underwear. I go on to do the same to the woman. As I remove her clothes, her gold necklace shimmers, taunting me. So I take it off, along with her heavy diamond-encrusted earrings. She won't look as good as I did in a leather jacket, but I can't leave her out here half-naked. So I dress her back up in my clothes.

Sometimes, I surprise myself with my moral compass. It's cracked, broken, and even shattered most of the time, but every once in a while, I'm capable of thinking about how my actions might affect someone else.

Her dress slips on as if it were custom made for me, and her heels fit perfectly. I clasp the necklace around my neck, throw my cheap TruMart earrings into the dumpster, and latch hers onto my ear lobes.

Staring down at her, I sigh. "You dodged a bullet tonight, sweetheart."

I run a hand through my hair, messing it up, flick my bra straps so that they hang off my shoulders, and loosen one of my heel clasps. Then, I turn away and walk out into the brightness of the city street.

As I come out, a man standing next to a brand-new candy apple red Camaro punches the air with this phone in his fist. "What the fuck, Jess? Where the hell are you? Why'd you leave your phone here? Fuck. She said she was right here."

Her boyfriend, I presume.

My timing is perfect.

Without hesitating, I stumble toward him, my messy hair making me look either high or like I've been attacked. My intention was to portray the latter, though admittedly, feeding does give me a high.

I can only hope he doesn't recognize the dress I'm wearing. If she's as snooty as I first thought her to be, she likely buys a new dress every time she goes out. He scans me from head to toe, so I flail my arms in a panic before he gets a good look at me.

"Please," I say, my voice heightening in pitch.

"There's a woman in there—" I point toward the blackness of the alley. "We... we were attacked. Please—"

Again with my kickass acting skills.

I don't even have to finish my sentence. His face blanches and he pushes himself off the door of his car before bolting straight into the darkness.

The moment he's out of sight, I run my fingers through my hair to remove the tangles, raise my bra straps, and refasten the clasp of my heel. With my chin raised high, I walk across the road, my hips swaying from side to side.

"It's showtime, motherfucker."

<h1 style="text-align:center">CHAPTER 11</h1>

The screeching sound of tires against asphalt reverberates around me as the BMW comes skidding to an immediate stop, its front bumper nearly knocking my legs out from under me. The young male driver shakes his fist behind his wheel, opens his window, and sticks his head out.

"Watch where you're walkin', you dumb bitch!"

With a single glare, I get him to retreat into the safety of his car like a turtle into its shell.

Fucking prick. He ruined my moment.

Rolling my shoulders back, I fix my dress and climb onto the sidewalk, next to a massive lineup that extends down to Tulip Palace—another famous club in San Halos.

People eyeball me as I approach the club, likely wondering how privileged I must think myself to be to walk up to the front of the line.

"Back of the line," the large, gorilla-shaped bouncer says without even looking at me. While that might sound like an insult, it most certainly isn't. The guy's ripped... like pro wrestler ripped, and if I wasn't in such a rush to get to Clock Dragon, I'd probably want a little taste.

"But you don't—" I start.

"Back of the line, no exceptions."

He puffs his chest out farther than his chin, then clutches at his tablet—presumably his guest list—and points at the line.

Why won't he even look at me? While I don't *need* eye contact to seduce men, it sure as hell gets things rolling.

"Wow, those arms—" I say, reaching for his bicep.

He jerks back, my fingertips barely grazing his rock of a muscle. "I'm not gonna tell you again, lady!"

It appears the nice approach isn't working. I guess it's time to bring out my bitch.

"Are you *blind*?" I say.

He huffs and drops his tablet against his waist. "Excuse me?"

His eyes hover over my head and still toward the line. What the hell is wrong with him? A succubus—the epitome of absolute beauty—is flirting with him and he acts like I'm nothing.

To me, that's more infuriating than an arrogant guy. At least arrogance can be knocked out of the way, but this guy won't even give me a chance. Inconspicuously, I sniff the air around me to get a good whiff of him.

Definitely a feeble.

What the fuck gives?

If I weren't a succubus, I'd think maybe he was gay. But with my beauty and my powers, sexuality means squat.

My frustration gets the best of me. "I said, are you *blind*?"

In an instant, another bouncer with bright orange hair and freckles to match steps out of the club and positions himself between the two of us. He places a large hand on the bulky bouncer's shoulder and another on his waist. "What the fuck is going on here? You're stalling the line."

"Your bouncer friend here refuses to look at me," I say. "That's awful client service if you ask me."

I must sound like a total whack job to the people waiting in line behind me, but I don't give a rat's ass. I have a job to do, and no one is getting in the way of that.

"The fuck is wrong with you?" says the redhead. "Derek's blind."

I point a finger at the sky and part my lips to defend myself, but something unusual happens... nothing comes out of my mouth.

Someone right behind me shouts, "Get in line!" and my shoulders jerk forward.

Seems I'm pissing everyone off.

"Listen," I say, reverting to my abnormally sweet self. "I believe there's been a misunderstanding."

Placing a hand on my hip, I jump to plan B and throw my Lure at the redhead instead.

He clears his throat, having obviously felt my energy, and shifts the weight of his body onto one leg.

That's my cue. I take a step toward him, making my hips sway out like a cat about to pounce and reach for his muscular forearm. "Listen, I'm terribly sorry for the misunderstanding. I've recently changed my hair, so it's understandable that you might not recognize me. But I'm certain you wouldn't want the media finding out that you denied Miss Vanpolis entry into your club, or that you made her wait in line."

I have no idea where I came up with that name.

"Oh, um—" he stammers.

The blind bouncer clears his throat, then moves his mouth over to his tablet and says, "Miss Vanpolis."

A woman's monotone voice responds, "No data found."

The redhead stares at me, and I stare back, refusing to back down.

"Sorry, Miss Vanpolis. I'm not sure what happened. Someone must have made an error. Please accept my apology on behalf of Rova Nightclub. Derek here will sign you in. Isn't that right, Derek?"

He squeezes Derek's shoulder, and that's when I realize his hand was there the whole time. My

Lure must have transferred over to Derek through the redhead.

Derek nods like a brainless goat and reaches for my hand. When I give it to him, he stamps the back with a red-inked stamp—a large V drawn inside a circle.

"Have a great evening, Miss Vanpolis," he says, his voice sounding different now.

I give them both a crooked smile, then turn my face toward the lineup as a way of saying, *And that's how it's done.*

As I enter the club, the music's loud beats send vibrations into my feet, up my legs, and into my head. Young men and women sporting noticeably expensive suits and dresses grind against each other with elegant drinks in their hands.

If I were to search the place, chances are I'd find celebrities I know. But none of that matters now. What's important is that I find Clock Dragon, so I can get a better understanding of what I'm going up against. This whole thing would have been so much easier if he'd stayed home. I could have snuck in through his bedroom window and taken care of business with no one ever knowing.

Blue, green, and purple lights flicker to the beat of the music and I blink, thankful I don't have a severe sensitivity to light. The club scene isn't my thing. I'm more of a dive bar kind of girl. Give me a pool table, a bottle of whiskey, and a few feebles to toy with and I'm happy.

As I make my way across the club, several glowing eyes turn my way.

Vampires... everywhere.

What the fuck?

"You look lost!" someone shouts over the deafening bass.

Turning around, I spot a young guy in a black silk button-up shirt, black dress pants, and shiny shoes to match. His dark blond hair is combed backward so perfectly you'd think he took an entire bottle of gel to it.

He smells fresh, so maybe he did.

"I'm not lost," I say.

His eyes search my lips, my chest, my legs.

I'm not even using my Lure, and I don't have time for this.

"Do you VD?" he asks, licking his lips.

"I'm sorry?" I say.

He pulls his face back and stiffens his posture as if he's revealed something he shouldn't have.

"Oh. Sorry." He twirls a finger around his ear. "I thought you were someone else."

He turns away, and I spot two bloody bite marks on his neck. I wrap a firm grip around his wrist before he takes off. "Where'd you get those?"

What I wish I could ask him is, *How the fuck are you still alive?*

He yanks away from me, his features hardening. "I don't know what you're talking about."

And with that, he disappears into the crowd.

How the hell is a feeble with fresh vampire marks walking around? Vampires aren't known for being merciful to their victims.

The deeper I enter the club, the more uncomfortable I become. Vampires eyeball me from every side, no doubt sensing that I'm fae.

Maybe this was a bad idea.

Or maybe I need a drink.

Leaning over the nearest bar I can find, I call the bartender over. A young woman with pale skin, perky breasts, and high cheekbones glides her way over as if traveling on an invisible skateboard.

Her eyes are cold and lifeless, and I can smell the rotten scent of death off her before her fangs make an appearance.

"Vodka," I say. "On the rocks. And not the cheap shit. Make it four drinks... In one glass."

Her arms move to reach for the booze under her belly, but her eyes remain glued on me. Still staring, she slides my drink across the bar and it lands in my hand. "We don't sell cheap... *shit*." The last word comes out of her mouth as if it's foreign to her.

Maybe it is. Who knows? She could be some cryptic bitch from the Middle Ages who was recently awakened to be hired as a bartender.

Nothing's impossible these days, especially in San Halos.

With the cold glass against my palm, I hesitate. Technically, I'm working, which means I shouldn't be drinking, but if I don't get some alcohol in my system, I'm afraid I might tense up and do something stupid. So I close my eyes and chug the cool liquid, enjoying every second of the fiery burn in my throat. Then, I dump the ice cubes into my mouth and crunch them like peanuts.

She's still watching me.

I'm tempted to tell her to go fuck herself—that sort of hatred only comes out when I'm dealing with a vampire—but instead, I point to my mouth as ice chips fall out. "Sexual frustration. Wanna help me with that?"

At last, she rolls her eyes and hovers away.

The moment I slam my glass back down, I catch a familiar whiff.

Clock Dragon.

He moves through the crowd with several gangster-like dudes around him and makes his way to a red velvet curtain. Some private room. It's protected by another handful of security guards with padded chests, broad shoulders, and hands larger than my face.

No way am I getting inside. It's one thing to work my Lure on a couple of bouncers at the front door, but it's quite another to manipulate my way inside some private meeting that's no doubt protected by countless guns and knives.

So instead, I lean back in my chair, trying to get a good look at Clock Dragon, but all I see is the back of his head before he disappears behind a brown-skinned man twice his size.

But these big guys aren't what I'm worried about.

What freaks me out the most is the man I spot at the end of a long, rectangular table. He sits with his fingers crossed in front of him, an elevated chin, blood on his bottom lip, and a cold gaze I'd recognize anywhere.

Lucius Retnich.

Chapter 12

This pain is not unlike being punched in the ribs by an ogre. The blows get rougher until at last, I'm shaken out of my dream.

"The fuck?" I say, cracking an eye open.

Next, the pungent smell of weed enters my nostrils.

Drax sits in front of me with bloodshot eyes and two thick arms crossed over his chest. "Seriously?"

Moaning, I wipe gunk from the corner of my mouth. "Seriously, what?"

"Where were you last night?" he asks.

Sitting up, I rub the back of my head, then glance down at my dress.

"Oh," I say.

"Oh? Alex, are you drunk?"

I flick a wrist at him and stand up, but catch myself on the back of the sofa before I tumble over. "Maybe."

"Maybe? Where'd you go?"

"I don't remember everything," I admit. "Went to Rova Nightclub—"

"Rova—" Drax starts, his reptilian eyes almost popping out of that snakehead of his.

"It's a long story. I went after the guy... You know. Him. Well, I followed him. Wanted to see what he was involved with."

"The guy who saw you in Adam Shaw's house?" Drax asks.

Is my drunken gibberish that bad? That's what I said.

I nod. "Yeah... Think I left after that. Went to another bar. Fuck. I don't know. I don't remember."

A vivid image flashes in my mind.

Lucius Retnich—slender, blond, high cheekbones, and long fingers that would make any piano player envious. He'd sat there staring straight ahead, tapping the large table in front of him as if trying to play a musical piece.

"Lucius Retnich," I say, staring at the floor.

Drax stiffens and slaps his hands on his hips. "Wait. What? You saw him? You sure it was him?"

He moves to the other sofa, sits down, cracks open a can of Pepsi, and lights up what remains of his joint. He puffs hard, smoke floating around his red eyes, and focuses on me as if I'm the only thing in the room. When I don't answer him, he relights the tip of his joint, inhales deeply, and coughs.

"Do you think I'm an idiot?" I say. "Of course I'm sure it was him."

He puts his joint down on one of my New York City coasters and raises his hand in submission.

"I'm just saying... The dude's been gone for how long now? Why would he be back? And what would he be doing in Rova Nightclub?"

Sighing, I throw my head back into my sofa.

Lucius Retnich used to run San Halos's Underworld, along with numerous surrounding cities. So what was he doing at Rova Nightclub? Is he back in the business? The guy's been around for centuries. Only last year, he disappeared. Rumors are he got sick of having to babysit everyone so he took off, cleared his name, and started a new life as most vampires do.

Some other vampire named Tyler Lorsan took over. What kind of vampire is named Tyler? It must be a new legal name. Either that, or he's *actually* a new vampire. A babypire, which is doubtful—leaders tend to be ancient motherfuckers.

There are countless leaders around the world, and each one reports back to the big guy... The king shit.

Asmodeus.

No one knows his last name.

He rules everything, and Lucius used to report to him, which means Clock Dragon is involved in some pretty deep shit. What were they doing inside Rova Nightclub, anyway? If Lucius is trying to regain the throne, something big is about to go down.

Should I be letting go of this? My specialty doesn't include investigating Vampire Mafia affairs.

I'm more of a kill and walk away kind of gal. Besides, I'm not even being paid for this.

"Maybe I should drop it," I say. "He obviously hasn't spoken to the cops."

Drax shrugs. "Maybe not. But you might've pissed them off."

I scoff. "I highly doubt anyone gives a shit that Adam Shaw is dead."

He shrugs again—a careless, overly nonchalant move that makes me want to throw a pillow at his face. "Well, I wouldn't be so sure about that. What if Adam was working for them? What if he owed them money, and now that he's dead, he can't pay them back?"

Glaring at him, I throw the pillow.

He blocks it with his scaly green arm and laughs—it sounds like an old gasoline-powered car failing to start.

"Why are you making this so complicated?" I ask.

This time, he shrugs a shoulder. "I'm not doing anything. You fucked this up, Alex. You should've killed the bastard when you caught him pointing a gun at you."

As much as I hate to admit it, Drax's right. I left a loose end and now I have to deal with it.

I make my way into the kitchen and start slamming cupboards. In the living room, Drax mumbles in a low tone.

"Your momma's crazy. Yes, she is. Yes, she is."

"Would you leave Mr. Mushroom alone?" I shout, tearing open my utensil drawer. Where the fuck did I put them? Next, I pull at the refrigerator door, hunch forward, and peek inside.

Of course—in the fridge. Where else would I have put my brand-new wrist strap blades? Shoving aside a six-pack of beer, I pull them out and wrap them around my wrists.

"What're those?" Drax asks.

Without saying anything, I smirk and snap my wrists downward, releasing the knives with a soft swoosh sound. To emphasize how cool they are, I kick the air and slice invisible demons around me.

"All right, that's pretty cool," he says. "But where are you going with those? I thought you didn't like using weapons."

Fighting the urge to glower at him, I retract the blades. The last thing I want to think about is what happened the last time I brought a sword to a fight. The kid was like a son to me. I don't want to picture his severed head... Drax knows that topic is touchy for me, and before I have the time to say anything about it, he shakes his head and mumbles, "Sorry, Alex."

"Shit's changed," I say. "Vampires are involved, and I need better protection." I pull off my dress, which smells like it sat in an alcohol chamber for months. Drax turns away as I search my apartment in my bare ass, looking for a pair of jeans to slip into.

I manage to locate a dirty pair on the floor,

along with a stained T-shirt.

That'll do for now.

Really, Alexis? You used to wear Gucci, Prada, and Louis Vuitton. Have some class.

Ignoring my judgmental inner monologue, I slip into my clothes and say, "Come on, let's go."

His cheeks inflate, and he nearly spits the Pepsi out of his mouth. "Go where?"

"To meet your friend," I say. "The one who exchanges information for money."

When he doesn't move, I give him my big *Does it look like I'm joking?* eyes and he hops to his feet.

"Do you have cash?" he asks.

I plant a hand on my hip and cock a brow. "Bitch, please. Thanks to Adam Shaw, I'm rollin' in money."

CHAPTER 13

"Check again!" I snap.

The woman behind the counter cowers, her silver-rimmed glasses nearly falling off the tip of her nose. In a croaky voice, she says, "I... I'm sorry, dear. I've checked three times. The system doesn't lie. You have a balance of four hundred and fifty-three dollars."

"This doesn't make any sense."

Dragging a trembling finger across her computer monitor, she says, "There are several transactions here..."

Drax clears his throat and glances at the lineup behind us.

I slam my fist on the countertop and the woman flinches. "Listen, lady. I had fifty thousand dollars in my account last night. How the f—" but I stop myself when a little kid starts crying behind me. I lean farther over the counter, and the woman slides her chair back a few inches. "Explain to me how that much money disappears in one night."

She points at her screen again and says, "Well...

I see a purchase here for eight thousand five hundred and seventy-eight dollars... Lunar Pub. Maverick's Steakhouse... three thousand four hundred and seventy-eight dollars. Then you have several more—"

"Just print me my damn transaction history," I say, hovering a threatening fist over the counter.

She nods, gets up from her chair with a hunched back, and walks over to the printer behind her. Returning, she pushes her glasses up her nose and forces a smile. "Here you are."

I snatch it out of her hand and her smile disappears. I realize I'm being a bitch, but I can't help myself. Who in their right mind wouldn't be freaking out if they found out all their money was gone? I quickly scan through the history details, but I'm too livid to absorb what I'm reading.

So instead, I wave the paper in front of her face. "Don't you people put daily spending limits on debit cards?"

"Typically," she says, "but you called us and asked—"

Behind me, a middle-aged man clears his throat and says, "Could you cut her a break?"

I swing around, fuming, and Drax tenses beside me. It's funny how Drax is twice the size of this man, but he's like a puppy—a gentle giant who despises any form of conflict or confrontation. That's not to say he wouldn't kill someone for me, but he wouldn't enjoy it.

"I'll cut you a break, old man. I'll cut your fucking legs if you don't stay out of my business."

I wave the paper in his face, and he pulls back as if I'm nothing more than an annoying mosquito. Behind him, a mother slaps two hands over her son's ears and gives me a death stare.

Drax clears his throat again. "Come on, Alex. Let's get out of here."

With nostrils flared, I glower at the man. I'm about ready to shove my fist in his mouth and tear out his intestines. I'm not proud of how angry I get sometimes, but when it happens, it's like I lose control of my own body.

"Alex," Drax says, resting his massive hand on my shoulder.

It's enough to calm me a bit, at least long enough to rationalize that beating an innocent man senseless in front of a bunch of citizens won't do me any favors. The guy didn't even do anything wrong—he's only trying to defend the poor old lady at the front desk.

But when my Red builds, everyone becomes the enemy.

Drax squeezes the back of my neck and I start to relax.

Without apologizing, I storm out of the bank with my statement in hand. The moment we step outside, Drax steals it from me and inspects every transaction.

"Are you kidding me? What did you do, Alex?

Buy out the fucking bar? And what the hell are all these purchases?"

I take the statement back, the paper snapping in the air, and crumple it up. "Doesn't matter. I don't have enough cash to see your guy."

But I remember something.

"Drax, where'd I put Adam's watches? The ones I brought home—"

"You came back for those last night, Alex. I have no idea what you did with them. You weren't making any sense. I tried to stop you from leaving, but you know how you get when you're drunk."

"Fuck!" I snap, punching the air in front of me.

"Alex—" Drax tries, whipping out his deep, comforting voice.

I raise a flat hand in front of his face and he seals his purple lips. Pulling my phone out of my jacket's front pocket, I flip it open and dial Jamieson's number.

The moment his voice comes through the speaker, I roll my eyes. "Darling! I knew you'd come around."

As much as I dislike his arrogance, I could listen to that accent all day long.

"I'm not coming around, Jamieson. I'm requesting another job."

"What for?"

I've never *requested* a job—the agreement has always been that Jamieson calls or messages me when he needs something taken care of. It's not my style to grovel for cash.

"For money, Jamieson, what else?"

Through the speaker, he shifts in his chair. "Love, did you not receive—"

I release a noisy sigh through my nostrils. "I received my pay. Something happened and I lost it, okay?"

"You *lost* it?"

I can see the smug smile on his lips from where I'm standing. It's not like this is a onetime occurrence. While I've never begged Jamieson for a job, I've accepted cheap ones more times than I can count to make my rent.

He must think I have a gambling problem.

When I don't answer, he says, "You do realize that my current offer would alleviate all of your financial problems, don't you?"

"I'm not taking that job, Jamieson!"

"Suit yourself," he says. His Italian leather chair creaks in the background. "But I don't have any other work for you."

"What do you mean—"

"Exactly what I said. I'm afraid I have to let you go."

He's toying with me.

"Jamieson! I need money."

He pauses. "How much do you need, Alexis?"

"Five grand."

He breathes out, and the sound of fingers tapping a solid surface enters my ear.

Why is he making such a big deal out of this? I've been working for him for several years now. Can he not do me this one small favor? He acts as if money is hard to come by when the guy's rolling in it.

Five grand wouldn't even make a dent in his wallet.

"What do you need it for?" he asks after a time.

"Information," I admit. "I'm in trouble, Jamieson. I can't talk about it over the phone, but I'm trying to get myself out of that trouble, and to do that, I need five grand."

"Tell you what," he says, his charming voice resurfacing. "I'll advance you twenty."

Is he messing with me? I'm surprised he isn't being a wise guy and telling me to sell the crossbow I stole from him. Like he said, it was a five-thousand-dollar weapon.

"Twenty dollars or twenty thousand?" I ask.

"Thousand," he says, matter-of-factly.

Tilting my head back, I gaze up at the clear blue sky and close my eyes.

While I want to be happy about this, I can't shake the feeling that Jamieson is pushing me into a dangerous corner. He's never offered me an advance before. The morning sun makes an appearance, warming my back. So I step aside and lean against the bank's exterior building.

"What's the advance for?" I finally ask. "You have another job coming?"

"I already offered you the job, Alexis. Take it or leave it."

With that, he hangs up.

Chapter 14

From across the street, a group of guys wearing bandanas, baggy pants, and guns shoved into their belts give Drax and me threatening glares. Turning away from them, Drax leads me down a small alley by the name of Petrie and alongside old wooden doors that remind me of the Middle Ages.

The walls of the building are made of mismatched gray stone and reach several stories up. Intertwined metal staircases are attached to the walls. They seem to lead from one apartment to the other down to the alley floor.

"Your guy works *here*?" I ask.

"He lives here," Drax says.

He walks up to one of the units with a rotting door, no windows, and a cheap dollar store sign that says, *No Solicitors*. He knocks with a pattern, no doubt some secret code meant to signify he's an ally.

"Keep your head down," Drax says through the side of his mouth. "And don't open your trap unless he talks to you. Got it?"

This is Drax's territory, so I shut my mouth and do as I'm told.

But the second the door opens, my jaw loosens, and I part my lips, thinking of at least a dozen jokes I could make.

In front of me is an ugly rock.

Well, a fae who must have some sort of rock ancestry. His eyes, two glossy black dots, sit somewhere deep on his horrific, deformed face. The bulk of his body, which comes up as high as Drax's torso, looks like it was made using beach stones and superglue.

With his soccer ball-sized hand on his door handle, he rolls his beady eyes up at Drax, at me, and back at Drax again.

"It's me," Drax says.

The rock man hesitates until finally, his face splits in half and hundreds of little rocks for teeth appear.

"Drax! My man," he says, his voice surprisingly high-pitched. I blink several times. It's hard to believe that such a squeaky voice is coming out of something like that. "Come on in, come on in," he says, gesturing at us to enter.

When he turns around, I'm drawn to the triangular-shaped rocks poking out of his back and along his spine—if he even has a spine. They remind me of a Stegosaurus's back. The moment we enter, he points at a small stone bench in his living room. "Have a seat."

Across from us, he pulls up a stool with a seat made of polished rock.

Oh, for crying out loud. Is everything in here made of stone? What about his fridge? Is that some giant rock? Or, better yet, is it full of rocks? Am I going to be offered a rock sandwich?

I sit down, the hard surface cold against my ass. Drax sits beside me, his elbow jabbing me in the ribs.

The rock interlocks its fingers, the scraping sound making me clench my teeth. "How can I help you, Drax?"

"Well, Georgius—"

Rock man waves a hand. "It's Kyle now."

"Kyle," Drax says. "My friend here is looking for information."

Kyle's creepy little eyes turn on me, but he doesn't say anything. I'm tempted to open my mouth and blurt everything I need information on, but I do as I've been told and shut my trap.

"Name?" he asks.

"Alexis."

"Full name."

"Alexis Rayne."

"Sounds fake. How many identity changes?"

I glance sideways at Drax. What's this all about? What does it matter how many times I've changed my identity over my lifetime? He either senses I'm a succubus, or he's that *good* at what he does.

"Twenty-eight," I say after a beat.

He nods slowly and rubs his chin, a cloud of fine dust sprinkling on his lap.

"You know the ways of the Underworld," he says.

Is he asking or telling?

"I expect you to keep my existence private."

I nod quickly. "I won't say a word."

His rocky brows move close together.

"Very well," he says, his mousy voice resonating throughout his weird-ass apartment. "Five thousand dollars is my fee."

"Yeah, after you tell me—"

"Upfront," he cuts me off.

Again, I look at Drax, who doesn't offer me much of anything. With eyes closed, he shakes his head as if to say, *There's no negotiating here. Either pay him or you get nothing.*

Fuming inside, I reach into my jacket pocket and pull out the envelope of cash I withdrew before coming here. He reaches for it, his huge fingers barely able to open the envelope, and starts counting what's inside. Finally, he leans the weight of his thick upper body onto his tiny knees. It astonishes me that they haven't shattered to dust with how heavy his body must be.

"What do you need?" he asks.

"What's Lucius Retnich doing back in San Halos? And who's Veerka Vanmorte?"

"My fee includes one question only."

Clenching my fists, I bite the inside of my cheek.

Why is he being such a jackass? It's two questions. Does he honestly expect me to pay him five thousand dollars per question?

I cross my legs and lean forward, then squeeze my breasts so that they look larger. "Come on, Kyle... I'm sure we can work something out."

I have zero intention of fucking a rock, but that doesn't mean I can't work my magic on him.

"Don't bother," Drax says, tapping my lap. "It won't work."

Clearly.

Kyle crosses his arms over his rock body and pouts, obviously unimpressed by my attempt to seduce him.

So which one is more important? Lucius or Veerka? Lucius is now involved with Clock Dragon, who is directly involved with me. Well, maybe. It's a risk I'm not willing to take. Veerka, on the other hand, is supposed to be my new mark, which sort of makes her the most important person right now.

The only problem is, if Clock Dragon and Lucius come after me, there won't be a *me* left to take out Veerka.

Fuck.

Kyle clears his throat—a grinding noise that makes me wince.

"Who's Veerka Vanmorte?" I ask.

Kyle leans forward and smacks his hard palms together as if preparing to share a campfire story. "She's new to San Halos. More specifically, she's new to the management team, if you catch my drift."

"I don't catch your drift, Kyle. I paid you five grand to give me everything you know—not beat around the b—" Drax nudges me and I stop talking.

"She's Lucius's new lover," Kyle continues. "Seems she's changing the game... Making new rules. Building a huge following. She's pushing for feebles and shadow dwellers to work together. At least that's what rumors say. Lucius denies the whole ordeal. Some people have even said she's after"—he lowers his voice to a faint whisper—"Asmodeus."

"So that's why Lucius is back..." I say, more to myself than Kyle. Then, I scoff. "Well, she's a delusional bitch if she thinks she can take out Asmodeus. The guy's been around for millennia. He's been in charge for as long as anyone can remember."

Kyle shrugs, his arms scratching his sides. "I'm a messenger, nothing more."

"Keep going."

"The two have been working together as a power couple. Tyler Lorsan hasn't been seen in three days, and rumor has it they've gotten rid of him."

I swallow hard.

What the fuck did I get myself into? And why does Jamieson want her taken out? Why is she such a threat to him? If I were to guess, I'd say it's because she's getting feebles to work for her when everyone knows that feebles are Jamieson's territory.

"It isn't my business to ask why you're inquiring about her," Kyle says, "but if you're planning something, I suggest you consider long and hard about how much you value your life before doing anything stupid."

CHAPTER 15

Refastening my leather cuffs around my wrists, I peer into the darkness of the alley.

"What're you doing?" Drax says, his voice a sharp whisper. "You heard Kyle. It's too dangerous."

"Relax," I cut him off before his eyes balloon out of his head. "I'm not going after her."

His chest puffs out like he's about to sigh in relief, when I add, "Not yet, anyway. Right now, I need to get rid of my other problem so I can focus on finishing my job."

"Alex—" he tries, but I don't stick around long enough to hear his speech.

Instead, I jump high up, expand my wings, and throw myself toward the night sky.

* * *

The old tube television flickers behind him, casting a blue light across his dust-covered blinds and the living room's shaggy carpet.

"It's all here," Ouru says.

He collects the paperwork together and straightens it out on his kitchen bar counter.

Scraping his claws along the hard surface, he slides it over to me.

"You sure you want to do this again, Rebel?"

"How many times do we have to go through this?" I ask, staring at him.

He smirks, flashing a set of crooked yellow teeth that protrude far over his lower jaw. His skin, a leathery brown, is so loose that he pulls it back from his face and ties it up at the top of his head like a ponytail, which makes his overbite look even more pronounced. "I'm just lookin' out for you, kid."

Ouru always means well, and every time I come to him for an identity change, he asks me the same question: "Are you sure you want to do this again?"

I'm never sure, but it's always a must.

He ashes his cigarette in a glass bowl in front of me.

"They killed him, Ouru," I say. "So I slaughtered the whole family... All of them. One by one. There's no going back from that."

Suddenly, the dry blood on my arms and neck feels hot against my skin. My clothes, too, are so stained you'd think I jumped inside a giant tub of red and black paint.

He nods, then reaches for my hand.

I pull away, wipe my cheeks, and glance down at the paperwork in front of me.

Passport.

Driver's license.

Birth certificate.

"Alexis Rayne?" I ask.

He nods and reaches for my hand again. "I'm so sorry for your loss."

I want to cry—I want to fall to my knees and tear my chest open. You'd think after losing so many people you care about, you'd become accustomed to it or you'd learn to cope better than the first time around.

The truth is, it doesn't get any easier.

If anything, it eats away at you more and more as the list keeps growing.

I took Jamal off the streets when he was nine years old—a kid born and raised in a neighborhood in the slums with dead parents and no chance at life. I gave him the chance he never had; I took him in and turned his life around.

I loved that kid more than anything. Although I thought of him as my own, he looked up to me as a big sister. So that's what I became—his sister.

He knew I was involved in something but didn't know what. And since he was a feeble, I wanted to protect him from it all. So the guns, the swords, and the knives in our apartment weren't to be touched or talked about.

Everything was going great.

That is, until I got jumped by a vampire in my own neighborhood. Killing him was easy, but that wasn't the problem. The problem was his pack. They found me... found out where I lived... and did to me what I did to him; they took away the one person I cared about.

I found Jamal's decapitated body when I came home after a job one evening. His lunch box was torn open, and the peanut butter and jelly sandwich I'd made him for school sat on his chest as if meant to signify something. Next to his body was my favorite sword—something I've held onto since the sixth century—covered in his blood.

They even shoved his head into his schoolbag—a painful reminder of his young age.

I swallow hard at the memory and focus my attention on my new documentation.

"Hopefully, I'll have better luck building a new life in San Halos."

Ouru smacks his colorless lips. "If you don't… You know where to find me."

* * *

"I'm not repeating history and starting fresh after only three years," I mutter under my breath.

The air around me is hot and humid—the kind of night that makes you wish walking around naked in public were legal. Using my elbow, I smash what's left of Adam Shaw's bedroom window—the one I dove through the other night—and climb inside. For the most part, everything looks as it did the night I was here. The only difference is his watches are gone and Clock Dragon isn't standing in front of me with a gun pointed at my face.

On the hardwood floor are circles drawn out in chalk. What are they circling? My footprints? The ones I left behind before jumping out the window? The cops are likely looking for fingerprints, though they'll never find them.

Pacing his room, I search every inch of space I can think of—under his mattress, in his closet, and even under his carpet. There has got to be something tying him back to Lucius. Why else would Clock Dragon have entered his home?

I'm a detective at heart, which means I need answers.

I don't find anything in his bedroom, so I make my way downstairs, where more lines are drawn on the floor. This time, it's in the shape of Adam's body.

I don't step too far out into the living room. Police cruisers are parked outside, guarding the perimeter of the home. If they see me creeping around inside, the cops will come in with guns in the air and backup on the way.

Adam Shaw's death isn't being taken lightly—that much is clear. There are many people connected to him in one way or another, and no one will be satisfied until the police blame someone for what happened.

For the police to immediately assume that foul play is involved means Adam already had a target on his back. Otherwise, my well-thought-out setup would have been enough to call it an overdose and close the case. Maybe I should've dumped his body in the river. Or maybe this is because I let the girl live. She may not remember who I am, or what I look like, but I suppose there's a slight possibility that she remembers that *someone* was with them that night.

Goddamn it. I should have killed her. What's wrong with me? I've never been one to hesitate when it comes to tying up loose ends, but ever since losing Jamal, I try to be a better person... for him... for his memory.

Clenching my teeth, I rummage through Adam's kitchen cupboards, his massive pantry that's meticulously organized, and through any door I can find.

Nothing.

I bow my head and sigh.

I'm wasting my time. He may have been a dirty piece of shit, but he wasn't an idiot. Whatever he was involved with, he knew how to keep it a secret from everyone. I'm about to head back upstairs and leave through the broken window when a sound captures my attention.

At first, it's a screech—like glass sliding across a concrete floor—but it turns into an inconsistent knocking. The sound gets louder, causing the floor to vibrate under my feet. Where is it coming from? The basement?

I head for the basement door and rest a hand on its handle. The sound continues, and this time, it tickles my palm. Bit by bit, I crack the door open and peer into the dark basement stairwell.

It's pitch black, but every few seconds, a flash of

green and purple light illuminates the bottom steps.

What the fuck is going on down there? Careful not to make any noise, I extract my blades from my cuffs and quietly make my way down one step at a time.

The flashes of light continue, which means whoever is down here doesn't hear me coming. With a hand resting against the staircase wall, I peek around the corner.

In the middle of Adam's basement—in front of a fully stocked bar, white leather couches, and an oversized jacuzzi hot tub—is a Serifus demon no taller than my waist with pointed ears, gray hair fastened in a bun, and raggedy clothing that looks like it was sewn together using material found in a mechanic's toolbox.

He hops up and down, holding what appears to be a wand. Whether he's dancing or performing some ritual is impossible to determine. He slams his wand toward the ground and all of a sudden, blinding balls of green light explode throughout Adam's entire basement.

"*Bag sagaris!*" he shouts.

Another flash of light.

What the fuck is this? The last time I saw a Serifus demon was over three hundred years ago. While they might be numerous, they're rarely seen by anyone in the Underworld. They're private people who tend to live underground.

Is this where this Serifus demon lives? In Adam's basement?

Out of nowhere, he stops swinging his wand around, bends forward, and glares at the shiny epoxy floor under his overgrown toenails. From here, I can see his face in the reflection—big yellow eyes, a long pointed nose, and a small mouth likely full of sharp piranha-like teeth.

If I can see his reflection, that means…

He swings around so fast his ears wiggle on either side of his head.

Shit.

"Traaa!" he shouts, pointing a clawed finger at me.

With his wand, he carves a large oval shape into the air, standing on his tippy toes to reach as high as he can. The air in front of Adam's bar crackles with flashes of electricity, twirling and distorting into what I can only assume is a portal.

Shit.

The little monster glances back at me, bares his incisors, and shouts "*Bagu!*" before running toward the portal.

Without thinking, I charge after him.

He dives headfirst into the portal and I do the same, squinting as I prepare myself to crash right into Adam's fancy wooden bar.

But there is no crash.

And everything disappears.

Chapter 16

"Riskus!"

The young girl raises a hand by her face, prepared to smack the Serifus demon in the head but stops herself when she catches me watching her. Her scowl quickly transforms into a forced smile.

How old is she, anyway? Sixteen? Her skin, a cool white, looks transparent compared to her port-red hair. Around her neck is a choker necklace with little silver crosses dangling all around. Although she's alabaster pale and has the whole goth look down pat, she doesn't smell like a vampire.

All right, that was a bit prejudiced.

Not all vampires look Gothic.

Her eyes, two bright green circles under dark, average-shaped eyebrows, shift between me and her demon pet.

"I'm sorry about Riskus," she says. "I have no idea how he managed to bring you here."

While I appreciate how considerate she's being

of my presence, I'm not exactly fond of the shackles around my wrists.

She catches me eyeballing them. "A precaution," she says. "I'm sorry about Riskus—"

She glares at her little minion and he cowers behind a bookshelf.

Where am I, anyway? I'm tied to what I assume is her bed—a double mattress with no frame and a black comforter full of long gray hairs. I take it the little monster sleeps on here. Beside me is a nightstand with an old wax candle that looks like it's never been used, a collection of witchcraft books, amulets, and multicolored crystals that probably came from the dollar store.

An amateur witch.

"Where am I?" I ask.

"New York City," she says matter-of-factly.

I roll my eyes. "I need to get back to San Halos."

Her jaw drops, a hint of a smile tugging at her lips. "I pulled you all the way from San Halos?"

She did this? And why is she so stunned? Is it because I'm right, and she's a total amateur? If there's one thing I hate as much as vampires, it's beginner witches—and yes, there are both male and female witches. Back in the day, the word *wicche* (that's middle English) wasn't gender-specific.

That's my lesson of the day.

Where was I? Oh yeah, the annoying beginner witches. They go around experimenting with magic

136

without a care in the world.

What the fuck was she thinking? I'm lucky to have made it through her stupid portal in one piece.

She hops onto her bed and slaps her knees. "Are you really from San Halos?"

She leans in, her bubblegum breath bouncing off my face, and I'm about ready to bite her nose off. She's chipper—way too chipper—to be a witch.

"I mean, I didn't think it would work," she says. "I've been practicing for days. I can't believe I actually sent Riskus to the amulet's location. Do you have any idea how hard I've been working on this—" She waves her hands energetically, and if her eyes were any wider, they'd likely dry to a crisp. "I had to find an infected toenail, rotten onions, damp garlic—"

"I get it," I say, rubbing at my wrists. "Can you take these things off me?"

I could easily snap them off with my super strength, but this kid looks too naïve. Chances are, she's never met a real-life demon, and I may end up giving her a heart attack.

With a smile still plastered to her face, she laughs awkwardly. "There's a little clasp—"

Of course there is.

I unclip the toy handcuffs and toss them across her comforter.

"They were on sale," she mumbles.

I don't say anything. If I do, it won't be nice.

"Listen, sorry about the whole transportation

thing—"

"I don't give a shit about that," I say, and she winces as if I spat in her face. "You need to send me back."

"Rachel, honey, supper's ready!" comes a woman's voice.

Her mom? Seriously? I'm about to snap at her for being so goddamn juvenile.

"Are you f—" but I stop myself.

She didn't mean any harm, Alexis. Cut her a break.

"What were you thinking? Playing with magic like this? Do you have any idea how dangerous this is? Do your parents even know what you've been up to in here?"

She gives me a sour look. "Um, duh. Of course, they know."

Her acting skills suck.

"My mom's the one who got me Riskus."

The elfin demon smiles up at me, his pointed chin resting in his little hands.

"All right," I say, sliding off her bed. "Well, since your mom already knows, maybe she has more experience and she can help us out."

I'm about to turn her bedroom door handle when she shouts out, "No!"

"Rachel!" her mother shouts back. "You get down here right—"

"Sorry, Mom! Not you. Um... Someone online."

Her mom doesn't respond, undoubtedly having

bought into her daughter's bullshit.

"Your mom doesn't know anything about this, does she?"

Rachel shakes her head.

"And you have no fucking clue how to send me back, do you?"

Avoiding eye contact, she mumbles, "No."

I'm about ready to punch a hole through her door and give her an entire speech about how young witches need to do their homework before trying to cast powerful spells—especially spells that involve traveling through time or space.

"Do you have any idea how much shit you've caused?" I say through clenched teeth. "San Halos is miles from here. How the hell am I supposed to get back now?"

She shrugs and raises her pierced eyebrow. "Um, I don't know. You could fly."

I laugh out loud and slap a hand on my forehead. "Fly? You want me to fly 500 miles? Are you insane? I'd never make it."

She pulls her face back and seems confused by what I meant.

"Would you keep it down? And what do you mean, you wouldn't make it? The airport isn't far from here. You could, like, walk."

"Oh, so you want me to buy a plane ticket because you're too inexperienced to send me back?"

"Look, I'm sorry, but I'm still learning."

I exhale hard through flared nostrils and point a finger in her face. "Listen here, you little witch. *You* used magic and somehow brought me here. So it's up to *you* to figure out how to send me home."

She crinkles her nose. "Home? That wasn't your house."

How does she know this? I pull away and tilt my head. She must sense my confusion and starts blabbering a bunch of stuff that doesn't make any sense, which leads me to believe she's trying to backpedal.

I cross my arms so tight that my jacket makes a squeaking noise. "I'm the adult, here, *Rachel.* I don't have to explain myself to you. You, on the other hand, sent your pet on someone else's property. So not only have you been recklessly using magic, but you're also breaking and entering."

"I didn't break—"

"Then you entered."

"Well, technically, Riskus—" she tries, but I cut her off with a flat palm.

"Why were you in there?" she asks, trying to match my pose.

"Like I said, I don't have to explain myself to you. It's a serious matter that involves a crime. The question is: why were *you* snooping around in Adam's house?"

The teenage attitude on her face vanishes in a moment and she smacks a hand over her mouth. "Oh my God. Are you a cop? Or... Or... a witch police?"

A witch police? Where would anyone come up with something like that? Teenage shadow dwellers have a habit of spreading all sorts of rumors when it comes to the Council of Elders. I'm tempted to play along—tell her that I'm a witch police and I've come to arrest her. But I don't.

"My friend Tracy at school warned me about the whole witch police thing," she starts rambling. "I thought she was messing with me. I figured—"

I take advantage of the situation. "She wasn't messing with you. Witch police are all around us."

She gulps hard, and although I feel bad for lying to a teenager, it's for her own good. She's going to get hurt, or worse, kill someone. Everyone knows that witches are supposed to be trained by an elder.

So where's hers?

"Is your mom a witch?" I ask.

She aims her face at the ground like she's about to cry. "I think my grandma was."

"Was?" I ask.

She nods. "She died a few months ago. I found those in her closet. I didn't mean to go snooping... Mom said the entire family was getting together to share her things, you know? I wanted the first pick. It sounds super selfish, I know. But I've never lost anyone before."

"Oh," I say. "I'm sorry."

"It's okay," she mumbles.

Although I should be comforting the girl, all I

can focus on is the pile of books on her bedside table.

"Those were hers?" I ask, pointing at them.

She nods.

"Can I take a look?"

Another nod.

All five of them are caked in dust. The one at the top, a small glossy black book with yellow pages, displays a crucifix symbol within a triangle. I'm not entirely sure what it represents—witchcraft isn't my specialty and I've never much cared for it—but it looks like something that shouldn't be toyed with.

"Does your mom know about these?" I ask, my finger leaving a streak through the dust.

"No... Are you gonna tell her?"

I glance up, and for the first time, all I see is a frightened child. We stare at each other for a few seconds, her green eyes resembling wet marbles, until at last, I say, "Your secret's safe with me."

I quickly scan through the smaller books—*Ancient Spells*, *The Art of Mastering Crystals*, *Demonology*—until I reach the bottom volume. The thing is so big it takes two hands for me to lift it off the table.

"Holy shit." I run my finger along the brown leathery surface. This thing looks like it was bound together during the early Middle Ages. Rusted metal buttons decorate the front cover's border, and four metallic strips run down the spine. The page edges are yellow and crisp to the touch.

The title is written in pre-Christian Latin, I believe. Running my finger across the engraved text, I gasp.

No way. It can't be.

How the fuck would some amateur teenage witch have the *Book of Origin*, the most powerful book in all of history, in her possession?

Chapter 17

Rachel cranes her neck, trying to read my expression. "What's wrong? What is it?"

I'm too intrigued by the book to pay any attention to her. Instead, I grab the corner of the cover and start pulling back.

Without warning, Rachel's hand lands flat on the cover, sending particles of dust into my eyes and up my nostrils.

"What the hell, kid?"

With a petrified look on her face, she shakes her head, which can only mean one thing: *You don't want to do that.*

I fight the urge to laugh. "Listen, there's no way this is the original *Book of Origin*. It's probably a good replica at best."

"*Book of Origin*?" she asks.

Maybe what I need to do with this kid is give her a good smack in the head. Maybe it'll knock some sense into her. How can she go around calling herself a witch if she doesn't even know about the *Book of Origin*?

She must sense my irritation because she starts babbling again. "I know it's important and stuff. When I opened it, weird things started happening in my room. I was about to look it up online yesterday. I mean, this is all new to me."

I'm tempted to say, *No shit this is all new to you,* but instead, I say, "Don't look it up online."

"Why not?"

I shake the book in front of her. "This thing has been hunted by witches throughout the world for centuries. The second you start googling this shit, you'll have all kinds of creatures popping up at your door to take it from you. Your grandmother must have been one hell of a witch."

A proud grin stretches her face. "Really?"

Now glaring at the front cover, I say, "Yeah. It's been missing for a long time, which means she must have concealed it with some powerful magic."

"So, what is it?" she asks.

"It's everything," I breathe.

This doesn't seem to satisfy her. She plops herself down onto her bed and punches at her pillow for added neck support. "What's the point of it?"

"It's a spell book," I say. "And a glossary. It contains everything anyone ever wanted to know about magic—the history of magic, a glossary of every known demon, and spells that are way too powerful for you to even consider trying."

Her eyes light up. "Sweet."

"No, not *sweet*," I say. "Do you have any idea how dangerous it is to have this thing?"

She frowns. "Well, I'm not getting rid of it. It was my grandma's."

Sighing, I place the book back down onto the night table. "You're putting your life at risk."

"I can handle myself."

There's no use arguing with her—her teenage hormones are too out of whack.

"Have you told anyone else about the book?" I ask.

It looks like she wants to say no, but I can see it all over her face: someone else knows.

"She's my best friend," she blurts out. "She won't tell anyone."

"How do you know?" I ask.

"Because she's my best friend."

I wish I could explain to her that she doesn't have enough life experience to understand that people are imperfect—that anyone can become someone else at any given moment.

"Listen, Rachel, I need you to be perfectly honest with me."

She swallows hard.

"What were you doing sending your little goblin to Adam Shaw's house? How did you conjure up the magic to do it?"

Reluctantly, she points at another book, the one with *Ancient Spells* written in cursive on the front cover. It looks about as old as the *Book of Origin*, only it's much smaller... small enough to fit in the back pocket of a pair of jeans.

Arching an eyebrow, I reach for the book. "Am I allowed to open this one?"

She nods.

The pages are crisp and white, but they're blank, so I slam the book closed. "Is this your idea of a joke?"

"What're you talking about?" she asks.

"It's blank, Rachel."

"No, it isn't." She leans forward to yank it out of my hands, but I pull away. "Page ninety-eight. It talks about the Heart of Danu... Some super powerful talisman. It had coordinates and everything on that page. All I did was google them until I found some fancy house on Google Maps. Then I found out it belonged to some rich guy. And then," she says, becoming even more lively, "I found out that the guy was killed, so I figured I wouldn't be hurting anyone by trying to find the talisman."

Without blinking, I stare at her. "Why are you trying to find a talisman? Honestly, it's like you're trying to get yourself killed." I flip the book open again and locate page 98. It's blank, too. I raise both eyebrows at her as if to say, *Page 98, huh?*

"It was there! I swear!"

"All right," I say. "Let's say I believe you... You still haven't answered me. Why do you want it?"

"Because it sounds super cool," she says. "It can amplify your power tenfold. You can do things others can't. It can even absorb magic... or something."

I scoff. "If this thing is as powerful as you say it is, you can't be the only one after it."

"I'm not." She looks down for a moment.

There's something she isn't telling me, so I glower at her until she breaks.

"Riskus overheard people in that Adam guy's house the last time he went. Like, a lot of people."

I'm about to cut her off and ask her how many times she's sent her little minion out on a treasure hunt, but I keep my mouth closed.

"Apparently people keep fighting in his basement. I guess when he died, the talisman made itself known. Well, that's what the book says. Once the owner passes, it sends out some sort of signal."

"You're telling me some feeb—some normal human guy had this talisman?"

She nods. "Why do you think he was so rich? It might not have brought him magic, but it made his life super awesome."

"Who else was in that house looking for it?" I ask.

She parts her lips to speak, but a squeaky voice fills the room instead.

"T-t-tall people," Riskus says. He balls his fists and rests his chin on them. His eyes, which are about the size of tennis balls, move between me and Rachel.

"It's okay," Rachel says. "You can tell her."

"V-v-very pale... Sharp teeth," he continues.

"Vampires?" I ask.

He nods so fast his little gray bun wiggles atop his head.

"Why would—" but I stop myself when it hits me.

That's why Clock Dragon was at Adam Shaw's house. He was looking for the talisman, and I'm willing to bet Lucius is the one who sent him on the hunt.

Clock Dragon isn't a threat—the talisman is. If anyone gets their hands on it and gives it over to Lucius and his new girlfriend, there's no telling how much damage that couple could cause in San Halos.

Chapter 18

"You sure this'll work?" I ask, staring at the swirling portal.

Inside is nothing but darkness, and around the oval shape, sparkling blue lights twirl so fast it looks like water. Riskus pokes his head inside but flinches when Rachel tells him to step back.

"It should work, but no, I'm not sure," she says. "It's worked the last four times with Riskus, but I've never tested it on a human before. I mean, it should work..."

Luckily, I'm not a human.

"That's reassuring," I mumble.

Suddenly, a knock against her bedroom door echoes throughout the room. "Rachel?" comes her mother's voice.

Rachel shoots me a frightened look, and I don't need to be a mind reader to know it's time to get my ass moving. As her bedroom door creaks open, I snatch the *Book of Origin* from Rachel's night table and jump headfirst into the portal.

* * *

Wooden panels snap and crack all around me as I come rolling through Adam's basement bar. The *Book of Origin* flies right out of my hands and lands in front of a man wearing glossy dress shoes, perfectly hemmed pants, and a white button-up shirt.

In the middle of his face are two yellow-brown eyes and above these, curved horns that stick out below his pointed hairline. His lips, plush and red, curve into the shape of a seductive smile under his pronounced cheekbones.

Who the fuck is this guy and why can't I stop looking at him?

"Interesting," he says, his voice hypnotizing.

Interesting? What's so interesting? I want to ask, but I inhale his crisp cologne like it's oxygen instead. Why can't I stop staring at him? His jawline, square and well-defined, makes me picture all sorts of naughty things.

I want him... more than I've ever wanted anyone.

What the fuck is happening here?

Then it hits me... There's only one explanation for this. The guy's an incubus.

Blinking hard, I fight my attraction to him.

"What do we have here?" he says, bending down to pick up the book.

Yeah, you bend down, big boy.

Shit. The book. He's about to grab the book.

Fuck. Stop it, Alexis. Focus.

He reaches for it, sharp claws digging into the cover's thick leather. They resemble mine, only they're much thicker and white.

"Don't touch that," I growl.

What was I thinking bringing such a powerful book into the portal with me? I'm a bit remorseful for stealing some kid's book, but it's far too dangerous for her to keep it. Some demon or witch would have easily cut off her head to get their hands on that thing. It's safer with me.

Hopping onto my feet and dusting chips of wood off my jeans, I say, "How'd you get in here, anyway? There are police everywhere."

I'm not sure why I'm trying to have a conversation with an incubus. Clearly, he's here for the same reason as everyone else—the talisman—and if I'm not careful, I might fall prey to his Lure.

Fuck that. He can try, but I'll make sure he's the one who ends up begging on his knees.

"What does this even say?" he asks, ignoring me. He raises the book to eye level and tries to read the Latin on the cover.

"Nothing you need to worry about," I say, though what I want to say is, *Who cares? Let's get our funk on.*

This only seems to intrigue him more. He's about to open the book when I smirk, igniting my Lure.

"Hold on, big boy."

He doesn't appear affected at all, but I have to

keep trying.

"How about we deal with this amicably?" I say, taking a step closer.

His eyes narrow on me and he smiles, almost arrogantly.

"A hot guy like you must have a pretty huge—" I peep downward.

As I move toward him, my horns come out and my hair lightens. This seems to excite him—he drops the book flat on the epoxy floor and lets both hands fall to his sides.

"Do you mind if I—" I point at his belt and he licks his lips.

With hips swaying from side to side, I make my way to him, slide the book aside with my foot, and slowly unclip his belt buckle. My eyelids flutter as his intoxicating scent fills me up.

Focus, Alexis.

The second I unbutton his pants, I feel a primal urge to throw myself at him.

Holy shit. This feeling is intense.

With eyes closed, I breathe out hard and inhale his scent. If I'm not careful, I'll end up wanting him more than he wants me, which could end up being my demise.

I'm about to unbutton my own pants when something totally fucked up happens.

All around us, flashes of red and white light bounce off the walls, across the ceiling, and throughout the entire basement. It's like being in an arcade, only without the constant dinging and acne-faced preteens kicking at machines.

I spin around to find a man with an oversized green cloak masking his face. At the tip of his drooping sleeve is a wand that appears to be firing lights like bullets.

The receiver of these light bullets is a hairy beast running at the other end of the room. His hair is so long that his eyes aren't visible, but he must be seeing the male witch with the wand—every few seconds, he dodges to the side, the witch's light bullets missing him by a millimeter.

Finally, the witch shouts something in Latin and a massive fireball the size of a smart car blasts out of his wand. The werewolf-looking creature doesn't have time to dodge this one. It hits him in the chest, sending him flying right through the wall behind him. Ceiling tiles fall from above and drywall dust fills the entire basement.

Suddenly, the witch's dark hood turns toward the incubus and me, as does his wand. The incubus glances at me and smirks—a look that says, *This isn't over*—then clicks his fingers and disappears.

What the fuck? Why can't I do that? A hot, searing pain on my thigh is enough to draw my attention back to the witch.

"Fuck, watch it!" I say, looking down at a melted patch of skin on my leg.

He points his wand at me again. This guy means business. I could lunge at him and snap his head off, but I risk getting torched and more importantly, I need to get the *Book of Origin* to safety.

"Why are you here?" he asks, his voice slow and calculated.

My eyes involuntarily dart toward the *Book of Origin*, and the second I do that, I feel like a fucking moron.

Why the hell would I look at the one thing I'm trying to hide?

His gaze follows mine, a slow turn of his hood.

If anyone will know how important that book is, it's a witch.

"Fuck it," I say, diving headfirst for the book.

The second I land on the cold floor with the book squished under my chest, another flash of blue light melts the skin right off my thigh.

The witch raises his wand again, prepared to fire another crippling blast when I catch sight of a two-by-four leaning against the wall. Grabbing it, I throw it at his chest with all my strength.

It sends him flying through the wall and into the cement foundation.

That's payback for burning me, asshole.

I immediately get up, bend my knees, and jump upward as hard as I can.

Ceiling tiles split, sheets of plywood snap in half, and hardwood flooring breaks apart as I tear through Adam's Shaw's house and land in his living room. Wrapped around me are cable wires I must have dragged up as I tore through the ceiling.

With my claws, I slice at the wires, trying to break free.

Below, the footsteps race across the basement and toward the massive hole I made.

As I free myself from the wires, a giant fireball blows up underneath me, lighting the hole on fire. The tips of my hair sizzle and burn off, but I roll away in time.

"Way to go, jackass!" I shout, pounding my fist against the floor. "Burn the house to the ground, why don't you?"

What is he thinking? If the talisman is hidden somewhere inside the house, or worse, underground, then destroying this place won't do anyone any favors.

At this point, the only thing I care about is getting the book to safety. As I kick away the last stubborn wire, heavy footsteps come barging up the basement stairs, so I dart through the kitchen, make my way up to the second floor, and run back into Adam's room.

The footsteps follow me, but I can outrun a witch any day.

With the book held firmly against my chest, I jump out through the window and extend my wings. Right when I'm about to flap them downward, a blinding flash disorients me, and something hard hits me in the back. I try to get away, but my wings aren't working. It's almost as if they're paralyzed.

And the next thing I know, I'm falling headfirst toward the ground.

Chapter 19

Branches and leaves scrape the skin of my bare ass as I climb out of the shrubs. That witch scorched off all of my clothes.

When I stand up, something feels off.

Why is everything crooked? Why am I staring at Adam's pool as if it were installed vertically on a wall?

Slowly, I reach for my face.

Damn it.

Where my forehead used to be is my right cheek. That prick broke my neck.

The pain doesn't bother me so much—it's knowing that if I weren't immortal, he would have killed me. That's enough to make me want to go back in there and tear his throat out with my claws.

But it's too risky. Besides, it's better this way—he'll think I'm dead, which means he might just leave me alone. With both hands, I grab my chin and the top of my head and yank sideways as hard as I can.

My bones snap back into place.

I'm about to jump into the air for takeoff when a sharp pain shoots from my ankle up to my knee.

Seriously? A broken neck wasn't enough? Looking down, I catch a glimpse of a bone sticking right out of my shin. With my other leg, I give it a good kick and it snaps back in.

The skin will heal over within a few minutes.

Now it's time to get the hell out of here.

I step forward, but my big toe smashes into something hard.

Where am I? A garden?

Around me are roses, tulips, hostas, and decorative statues lined up against a brick wall. Throughout the fresh red mulch are three garden gnomes—the famous proverbial principle of *see no evil, hear no evil, speak no evil.*

The three gnomes wear green pointed hats and have stone gray beards full of intricate designs. Their bright blue shoes stand out the most.

While all three of them are astonishing to look at, it's the gnome who represents *Speak no evil* that draws me in. His eyes, two blue sapphires, glimmer under the moonlight's glow as I move closer. For a moment, the left eye shines a faint pink, and I find myself wanting to pluck it from its face.

Whatever that is, it isn't a decorative eye.

It couldn't be what everyone's looking for, could it? Would it be hiding in plain sight like that?

Rubbing my chin, I realize that if this is the Heart of Danu, then hiding it in his garden may have been the smartest thing Adam Shaw ever did. Who would think to look here?

I bend down and reach for the gnome when a witch's voice echoes behind me.

"Stop right there."

Well isn't this awkward? I'm bent over, my bare ass giving him a free show, and I imagine his wand is aimed right at me—his magical wand, I mean.

"Stand up... slowly."

His voice sounds strained, and I'm betting it's because I broke a few ribs with that two-by-four. Serves him right.

If he thinks I'm submitting to his commands, he's delusional. I'm getting out of here with the *Book of Origin* and the Heart of Danu. The question is... how?

If I grab the gnome and take off, chances are he'll shoot me right out of the sky again.

So instead, I grab the *See no evil* gnome and in one hard swing, throw it straight at the bastard's head. It explodes into hundreds of pieces the moment it hits his face, and he stumbles back with arms flailing in front of him.

I snatch both remaining gnomes and launch myself into the air. Below, he reaches for his eyes, no doubt trying to dig out pieces of gnome, and for good measure... I throw the *Hear no evil* gnome at the top of his head.

He stiffens like he's about to keel over and I laugh. "Bet ya didn't see that coming, motherfucker!"

* * *

With the *Book of Origin* in one hand and Adam's gnome in the other, I land on the rooftop of my apartment building. While I shouldn't make a habit of entering my place through the roof's emergency exit, sometimes it's the only way to go about it.

When I enter my apartment, Drax is standing in the kitchen, frying himself what smells like a grilled cheese sandwich.

"You're home," he says, his voice tight. "Where the hell have you been?"

Panting, I ignore him, rush into my bedroom, and start scavenging through my closet. I manage to slip on a pair of pants and a hoodie before Drax sees me naked. Personally, I don't care who sees me naked, but I know it makes him uncomfortable.

He follows me with his sandwich in hand and Mr. Mushroom clawing at his leg. Mr. Mushroom's jaw snaps shut and he swallows hard.

"Did you just feed my dog?" I ask, looking over my shoulder.

"No," Drax lies. "What're you looking for? And what do you have in your hands?"

"Something I shouldn't," I admit, kicking aside a pile of three-week-old laundry. I plow through a bag of giveaway clothes, a comforter I never use, and a box of shoes and leather boots I have yet to organize.

"There you are," I say, reaching for my metal

chest.

After being emotionally exhausted by that witch and shot in the ass by the other witch, I don't have the energy to pull it out. So instead, I open the cover and toss the *Book of Origin* and the gnome inside. The gnome shatters, not that it matters. What's important is what's attached to its eye.

Behind me, Drax swallows the rest of his sandwich and cranes his neck. "You're using your Cloak Chest? You haven't used that thing in—"

"Yeah, I'm using it," I say sharply.

Slamming the lid shut, I snap the latches and lock the five different bolts into place. I stole this chest—something known as a Cloak Chest—a few decades ago from some independently owned witchcraft shop in downtown New York.

Looking back, stealing from a witch might have been idiotic, but I didn't have any money yet, and I needed to hide a relic I also stole from the shop. It appears the magic surrounding this chest hides any item inside from any form of tracking or locating spells.

I let that relic sit in there for about five years before selling it to a Gorton demon. I made a pretty penny, so the wait was worth it.

"What's so important you have to conceal it with magic?" he asks.

I straighten out, plant both hands hips, and let out a sharp breath. "The *Book of Origin.* Oh, and the Heart of Danu."

His hairless brows almost touch. "You're joking, right?"

"Wish I were, Drax. It's a long story. Some little witch pulled me out of San Halos. I found this book in her room, so I took it. It belonged to her dead grandmother. It's not like she needed it. It would have gotten her killed. If you ask me, I did her a favor. Then this witch tells me about the Heart of Danu, some super powerful talisman she traced back to Adam's house... And, well, I found it at Adam's house. A total fluke. I was more interested in getting out of there with this book. I can't believe I managed to find the talisman, too. What a night."

I raise a fist to offer a toast with my invisible glass of wine.

Drax's mouth flattens into a straight line. "You stole from a kid?"

"A teenager," I respond. "And, yeah, I did. That thing's too dangerous for her."

This is a new low for you, Alexis.

"But it's safe for you," he says, "a demon who knows nothing about magic."

Scowling at him, I straighten my stance. "I've been around long enough to know a thing or two about magic."

A thing or two is pretty spot-on.

He scoffs. "You know *about* magic. You're not a witch, Alex. Magic isn't your specialty. And I can't believe you stole—"

"Can you find me a buyer? I bet I can make a lot

of money off this."

"For the book, or for the talisman?" he asks.

I brush past him and make my way over to my bottle of Dragon's Tear. "Both. And not now. Let's wait a few months. But I'll take a down payment." I pop the cork and take three shots worth.

He doesn't seem too impressed with me. Tilting his head, as if this will somehow allow him to better understand how my brain operates, he crosses his thick arms over his chest. "Let me get this straight... You stole some kid's book—"

"Teen."

"Some teen's book... Something that meant a lot to her. Then she tells you about this talisman, or whatever... something she's been trying to find for herself, and you steal that, too."

"Technically, I didn't steal it." I point a finger upward. "It used to belong to Adam Shaw, and now that he's out of the picture, it was anyone's game. And to be honest, I'm the reason he's gone, so it's only fair—"

"You stole to make a profit," he cuts me off. "Which one is it, Alex? Do you even care about protecting this kid, or was it all for the money? If this thing is so dangerous, why the fuck would you want to put it back out into the world?"

I stare at him, then shift my eyes to the side as if to say, *Am I missing something, or are you a total moron?*

"Um, yeah... I steal, Drax. You know that. Why

the fuck else would I take it? It doesn't do me any good."

I realize that in one breath I said stealing the book was about protecting Rachel, and in another stated I wanted to sell it to make a profit. Sometimes, I even confuse myself. Especially lately. Squinting my eyes, I take a good look at the bottle of whiskey in my hand.

Did I take more than three shots?

Drax's jaw loosens. I don't get why he's so upset about this. I've done far worse things than steal a goddamn book and some fancy little gem.

"I don't know, Alex." He shakes his head. "For a second there, I thought you were being honest when you said you took it to protect the girl from getting hurt. Then, I hoped maybe the deeper reason was that you'd taken it to protect the whole world from being fucking obliterated by some maniacal witch." His tone becomes sharp. "Or did you even think about that? Did you ever stop to think about the damage that book and talisman could cause in the wrong hands? You'd think after going what you went through—"

"This is business, Drax. Besides, you're overreacting. Find a decent buyer, and we'll be fine. All I care about is paying my bills on time."

"You have a five-million-dollar job!" he shouts, shaking the walls of my apartment. "What more do you want?"

I put the bottle of whiskey down before it

cracks in my fist. "I'm not doing that job."

"You told Jamieson—"

"I know what I fucking told him, okay? I needed the advance, that's it. So find me a goddamn buyer so I can pay him back the advance and drop the job."

With nostrils flared so wide they take on the shapes of ovals, Drax sucks in a slow, calculated breath. His chest heaves like it's on the verge of exploding and his eyes turn into menacing yellow slits.

He rarely gets mad, but when he does, it's scary and I know I've crossed a line. But I'm not the type to back down, even against him.

So I stand there, glaring back as Mr. Mushroom cowers away and plops down onto his memory foam bed.

"Go find your own buyer," Drax growls, throwing something small and hard at my face.

I catch it before it hits me in the eye and open my palm to find a key... What the heck is this? It's encased in a black plastic shell and has a red triangular-shaped button that reads, *Ducati*.

"What's this?" I ask.

With gritted teeth, he says, "Your drinking problem."

<h1 style="text-align:center">CHAPTER 20</h1>

The power in this thing—the satisfying purr between my legs—makes me want to feed.

With a spin of the handle, I take off through the streets of downtown San Halos, zooming past cars and flipping off those who honk at me. There are a handful of reasons why I could get pulled over for riding this bad boy, including my inability to obey speed limits, but I don't give a shit.

Let the police try to catch me. It wouldn't be the first time I evade the cops on a motorcycle. It's become a bit of an art, and I have yet to get caught.

I drive for hours until traffic lightens and stores start locking their doors.

Finally, I reach Gray Stone Park—San Halos's most hidden gem, in my opinion. During the day, the place is shaded with hundreds of sugar and flower bushes that run along the San Halos river.

At night, however, most people avoid the place. It tends to fill up with the kind of people most noble citizens try to avoid. Some nights, when I can't sleep or when my mind's racing a mile a minute, I come here.

Okay, I fly here, which I should stop doing, but now that I have myself a shiny new bike, I'll be able to come more often without the risk of being spotted in the sky. I park my bike next to a weeping willow tree, turn off the ignition, and slip the key into my back pocket.

The air around me is fresh and crisp, and the cloudless night sky lights up the tops of the trees with thousands of floating stars. I make my way along the stone path and breathe in the river's cool scent.

In the distance, a few rowdy young guys heckle each other, no doubt drunk out of their minds. While drunken guys tend to cause trouble for me, they aren't difficult to deal with. A few elbows to their noses is enough to send them packing.

It's still annoying, though, and I'm not in the mood tonight. Luckily, they're standing under the park's pedestrian bridge and nowhere near where I'm headed.

Right now, all I want is peace and quiet so I can figure out what the fuck to do about this Veerka woman, Clock Dragon, and the new items I've collected. Closing my eyes, I tune out the rambunctious group and instead, focus on the sound of my feet against the ground, leaves rustling overhead, and crickets singing in the distance.

For a moment, a sense of calmness washes over me, but all of that vanishes when I hear something that's far from peaceful. From the river's bend comes a woman's shrill cry. I've heard that sound more times than I can count in my lifetime—it's the cry of someone who's being attacked.

It's not your business, Alexis.

People get attacked in San Halos all the time. Why is it my job to save them? I'm not a cop. I have better things to do.

You really are selfish.

I grind my teeth at my inner dialogue. Being selfish is what's kept me alive all this time.

Selfish.

Irritated, I empty my lungs and dart toward the woman. She screams again, and the sound of skin slapping skin echoes throughout the park.

I approach a group of six or seven men and women standing in a circle with rounded backs and mouths wide open. A terrifying growl escapes the tallest of the gang, and he moves into the circle, his pale skin and blond hair looking white under the overhead lamp post.

He reaches down and the woman screams again, but this doesn't seem to bother him. Abruptly, he yanks upward, lifting her into the air by her frail wrist. She kicks back and forth, her mouth a gaping black hole.

Then, with a devilish red glow in his eyes, he opens his mouth so wide it's a wonder his jaw doesn't unhinge. The woman squirms and squeals like a mouse as his sharp, glistening fangs move toward her neck.

Fucking vampires.

How is this even possible? Asmodeus has a strict policy regarding vampires and visibility. Vampires are always to remain out of sight and they are forbidden from feeding off humans unless those humans are raised in an underground feeding farm.

That's been the law since 1939.

"Hey!" I shout just in time.

Slowly, he turns his head, a menacing purr slipping past his lips.

At the same time, the rest of the vampires turn on me, their lips pulled back over their fangs. I realize that I'm doing what I swore I'd never do again—confronting vampires. But how can I not? They're about to tear her to shreds. Although I try to convince myself that I don't give a shit about feebles, I can't sit around and watch one be mauled to death.

I take a step toward them. "Let her go."

Without breaking eye contact, the leader of the vampire pack throws her onto a bed of pine needles. She whimpers as she lands hard on her back, but I'm too preoccupied with the vampire moving toward me to worry about her injuries.

I'm suddenly reminded of the vampires I slaughtered after Jamal's death.

"You're about to make my day a whole lot better," I say through gritted teeth.

I reach for the nearest branch I can find, tear it right off the tree, and snap it in two. It breaks apart sharp enough to mimic stakes, and the second they're close, I whip out my wings and reveal my true self.

Three of them take a step when it's clear I'm not some little feeble.

The tallest of the pack comes at me first with a bowed head and balls of blood for eyes. He frowns, his furrowed brows darkening his face even more. I have no doubt he's the strongest of the group. Once I take him out, the rest of these cockroaches should be pieces of cake.

I'm about to lunge straight at his chest with my handmade stakes when he flickers and the next thing I know, my throat is being squeezed by what feels like vise grips and I'm dangling in the air. His grip is so powerful that my arms go numb and I involuntarily drop my stakes.

Son of a bitch.

I try to breathe, but nothing enters my nose or mouth. If I don't do something fast, he'll keep squeezing until my head falls off, and if there's one thing that'll kill me for good, it's losing my head.

In one swift motion, I shoot my wings out on either side of my face and with my wing claws, pierce his eyes. He drops me and roars as tears of blood leak down his powder-white face.

I land with a loud thump, a blast of wind blowing away from me. Now blind, the vampire spins in circles, trying to listen for my footsteps. Behind him, his pack hesitates. It's like they want to protect him, but they know better than to undermine their leader.

I don't give them enough time to make a decision. Extracting my wrist blades with a loud snap, I use my wings to propel myself straight at the vampire. He tries to swat his claws at me, but I'm too fast, and he misses.

Infuriated, he growls loudly, but his voice cuts the second I tear my stakes into his neck. With a scissoring motion, I pull them out sideways, severing his head in an instant.

Cold blood spits out onto my face as his head falls onto the stone path with a loud thud. It rolls toward the rest of his pathetic followers, and right before hitting their feet, explodes into a ball of dust, along with his headless body.

Smiling, I twirl my long bloody stakes in my hands. "Why are you all just standing there? Let's party."

The first vampire to hiss at me is the first to receive a stake through her heart. She clutches at the wood sticking out of her chest and slants her brows before bursting into fine dust.

The vampire on the opposite side of the group— a young hipster with shaggy hair, baggy pants, and small canine teeth—looks mortified. He stumbles on his own feet and starts running down the path in the opposite direction.

If there's one thing I can't allow, it's for word to get out that I massacred a family of vampires... again.

"Not today," I say, throwing my second stake right past the vampires' faces and straight into the hipster's back. The force of the impact sends him whirling into the air with flailing arms. Right before he crashes into the ground, he dissipates into oblivion.

In front of me, three vampires remain—two males and one female. Only moments ago, the three of them had ferocious scowls aimed at me. But now, they shoot each other uncertain looks, seeming to have lost all confidence in their ability to fight me.

If they think I'm letting them get away, they're dumber than they look.

"Should've left the feeble alone," I mutter.

Before they can even attempt to run the other way, I move toward them at lightning speed, my arms sticking straight out on either side of me. My wrist blades decapitate the two males, and dust falls to the ground like ash from a burning barn.

Retracting my blades, I blink hard and slap the dusty air in front of me.

By the time the dust settles, the female vampire is already half a mile down the stone path.

She may be fast, but so am I.

With two arms sticking straight above my head like a superhero, I kick the ground and tear through the air, my wings launching me at a speed far greater than hers.

She shrieks when I grip my claws into her back, flap my wings, and elevate her into the air with me. Kicking her legs, she struggles to get back down, but it's no use. If she thinks she can escape me, she's delusional. I wrap my legs around her waist and squeeze tight, holding her captive. She tries to squirm, but if she tries too hard, she'll only end up breaking her own bones.

I pull my claws out of her back and stab them deep into her neck. Silky blood slips down my fingers as she gurgles black blood. I dig my fingers even deeper, and push upward as if removing the cork of a champagne bottle.

Her head pops and spins down toward the San Halos river, bursting into a thousand pieces. Her body does the same, her ashes sprinkling down on the water like fish food.

I flap my wings to stay in midair and gaze down at the frightened feeble. She sways back and forth with her arms locked around her legs and her face dug into her knees.

There's no doubt in my mind that she saw the entire thing.

Fuck.

What am I supposed to do about her?

That makes another loose end, and not cleaning up loose ends got me into all this trouble in the first place. Inch by inch, I lower myself to the ground, tuck my wings, and hide my demon self. I walk toward her and she pulls away the moment I kneel.

"Hey," I say.

With eyes still sealed, she shakes her head vigorously as if trying to erase what she saw. Either that, or she's terrified I'll do the same thing I did to them.

When she doesn't look up at me, I grab hold of her arms and she flinches.

"Listen to me," I order.

Reluctantly, she cracks her bright eyes open.

The moment we make eye contact, she freezes, and I realize I can tie up loose ends without taking or threatening to take a life.

Smiling, I brush her hair behind her ear and project my Lure onto her.

"Who... who are you?" she stammers.

My fingers make their way across her jaw, her lips, and her neck.

A man attacked you, I say with my mind. *I saved you. Nothing more.*

"What... What happened? I saw—"

You were drugged at a bar, I project. *You suffered hallucinations.*

She bites her bottom lip and glances toward the piles of ashes, so I squeeze her chin and force her to look at me.

"I scared the man off," I say aloud. "You have nothing to worry about anymore, okay?"

She nods, hanging on to my every word.

With her chin still in my grasp, I move in and press my lips against hers. Her entire body relaxes and she breathes out into my mouth.

Part of me knows I should be getting rid of her, but I can't bring myself to do it. I may be a bitch, but I'm not a *total* monster. She's the victim in this. If I kill her now, what would have been the point in saving her in the first place?

I pull away, and she gapes straight ahead as if hypnotized.

Without another word, I get up and walk back toward where I parked my bike.

Chapter 21

"I didn't do anything," Drax says, raising his hands to either side of his face.

This is what he says every time he *does* do something. So, what is it this time? It must be pretty bad if he's back here in my apartment. Only hours ago, Drax stormed out. The few times he's done that, it took a few weeks before he resurfaced.

I throw my key on the kitchen counter and head into the living room.

"What did you do this—" I start.

"You're a thief," comes Rachel's voice.

She stands in the middle of my living room frowning. Next to her is little Riskus. He puffs his chest, crosses his bony arms, and matches his master's expression. If he were wearing shoes—or more importantly, if he wasn't standing barefoot on my floor with those monster feet of his—he'd likely tap his foot to emphasize how upset he is.

"What the fuck are you doing in my apartment?" I snap.

Her eyes narrow, almost disappearing into her

face.

"You stole my book," she says.

I fling my hand out at Drax. "Why'd you let her in?"

"I didn't," he says.

"I've been practicing my portals to track you down," Rachel says.

Is this kid for real? "It hasn't even been twenty-four hours!"

"I practiced a lot."

She refuses to look away, so I place a hand on my hip and shift my weight onto one leg to project the same level of attitude. "What do you want?"

She gives me a stupid look that says, *What the hell do you think I want? A cookie?*

"My grandma's book!"

I smirk. "How much you got?"

"How much—what the hell are you talking about?" she says.

"Here's the thing," I say. "That thing could set me up for life... if you catch my drift."

Her face darkens three shades of red. "It's not yours to sell!"

I can sense Drax's disappointment from here, but I ignore it.

"Maybe not ethically," I say, "but I'm the one who has it now. So if I want to sell it, there's nothing you can do to stop me."

Her features twist so disproportionality it looks like she's about to cry. God. I hope she doesn't. I hate being around people who cry.

With pouty lips, she pulls a wand out from under her jacket and points it at me.

I raise my eyebrows. "Oh, so you're going to use magic on me, are you?"

"If I have to."

Riskus pumps a fist in the air and gives me a look so menacing I imagine he's preparing to maul my feet.

"Alex," Drax says, "just give her the damn book."

"No!" I shout. "I already told you. I need cash to pay Jamieson back."

"Sell your new bike," Drax says.

I ball a fist, prepared to knock his teeth down his throat. No fucking way am I selling my new bike. Besides, I don't even know how I got it. With my luck, I'll end up trying to sell it to the person I stole it from.

"Not gonna happen," I say. I realize I'm being unfair to this girl, but when I feel cornered, I have a habit of lashing back. "And stop trying to push me into taking that goddamn job. I'm not doing it. It's suicidal. And that vampire bitch is impossible to get to. Short of being able to walk through walls—"

And then I realize something. I may not be able to walk through walls, but I now know something who does.

"Rachel, sweetheart," I say.

Drax releases a loud grunt. "For fuck's sake, Alex, she's a minor."

"Oh, would you relax? *Sicko*. I'm not trying to seduce her. I'm being nice."

Is the idea of me being nice *that* unrealistic?

Rachel wrinkles her nose. "Ew. Seduce me? What the hell are you talking about?"

"Rachel, honey," I say, taking a step toward her.

She jabs her wand in the air as if to say, *One step closer and I'll turn you into a frog!*

"There's so much you don't know," I continue. "For one, I'm not human." My horns come out and my wings expand so far their leathery skin hits Drax in the face.

Rachel's jaw drops.

"Did you honestly think you were the only special person out there?" I ask.

"I-I-I," she sputters.

"I'm a demon," I say, not wanting to go into the specifications of my kind. "And there are plenty more out there. Some far less attractive than me, of course..." When no one laughs, I continue. "There are vampires, too."

Slack-jawed, she says, "Vampires?"

Slowly, she turns to Drax as if expecting some huge transformation. Being that she's an amateur witch, she sees Drax the same way feebles do—as an average, scrawny guy. As her powers develop, so will her ability to see fae in their true forms.

"There's so much you don't know," I say, "which is why I don't feel comfortable giving you back such a powerful book."

The shocked look on her face hardens into her earlier scowl.

"Let's make a deal," I say.

She doesn't look impressed, but it's obvious she's willing to hear me out. "What kind of deal?"

"You help me by using a bit of your magic, and in return, not only will I give you back your stupid book, but Drax here will arrange for you to get an apprenticeship with one of San Halos's teaching witches."

Her eyes go huge and a silly grin widens her face. "Really?"

Drax gives me the stink-eye. "And why would I do that?"

"Because you're a good demon," I say, taking advantage of his soft side. "And this little witch needs a mentor if she hopes to survive in this world."

"So find her one," he says.

It isn't like Drax to deny someone help—especially someone as young and innocent as Rachel. It's obvious this has nothing to do with her and everything to do with me. He's still upset by how I handled the book and talisman situation.

Despite my track record, he's always pushing me to be a better person. So when I become an uber bitch, or self-involved, it upsets him.

Rolling my eyes, I let out a sigh. "I'll give her the talisman, too."

"Talisman!" Rachel shouts. "What? How—"

"Shut up, kid," I say, staring Drax down.

Then, Riskus hops up and down. "Talisman! Talisman!" His squeaky voice hurts my ears, making me want to kick him into the air.

It takes a few seconds, but Drax gives in at last and nods, though it's obvious he wants more.

What the fuck more could he want?

"What do you want, Drax? An allowance?"

He shrugs his green scaly shoulders and smirks.

Finally, I throw my arms up. "All right, I'll take the job and give you a cut of my damn payout."

CHAPTER 22

"I think my mom would kill me if she knew I was here," Rachel says.

We walk straight through Clock Dragon's rough neighborhood, careful not to run into someone looking for trouble.

"Where does she think you are?" I ask.

"In bed."

Only then do I realize it's past midnight.

Right," I say, matter-of-factly. "Then we'd better do this quick before morning comes."

While this neighborhood is no place for a girl her age, she's safe by my side. Besides, if she's going to create a portal to get me to Veerka, she needs background information, and she'll likely need a few unconventional ingredients.

The moment we reach Clock Dragon's weed-ridden front lawn, a dog barks at us from across the street. He doesn't shut up, inviting other dogs across the neighborhood to join in.

I lead Rachel up Clock Dragon's concrete steps and smirk back at her. "Some dogs don't like my smell." I glance around to ensure no one's watching, then press my body against the door and turn the handle. "It's locked."

Rachel doesn't seem too bothered by this. If anything, it seems to excite her. "Perfect! I've been practicing a door unlocking spell..."

From her inner coat pocket, she pulls out her wand and aims it at the locked handle. "*Lucia palus.*"

A soft click echoes from the other side.

"Not bad, kid, not bad."

Turning the handle, I step inside. While I'm certain Clock Dragon is out doing some important vampire business, I can't be too cautious. We sneak in as the scent of mildew, three-day-old macaroni, and rotting cheese intoxicates our lungs.

I'm willing to bet this family's been living off cheap pasta for a long time. Maybe that's why Clock Dragon's involved with Lucius... To earn extra cash.

The lights are off, making our exploration taxing. As we move deeper into the home, a blue light flickers from down a hallway.

A television?

"Come on," I whisper, "the girlfriend's probably—"

A woman's scream pierces the silence, bouncing off every wall. Out from the darkness comes a fast-moving figure charging at us. In her grasp there appears to be a large kitchen knife, its point aimed right at my face.

From her perspective, she may be moving fast enough to take out her attacker.

From my heightened perspective, however, she's nothing more than a frightened feeble moving at the speed of a sloth. The moment her knife comes stabbing in a downward motion, I slip sideways without any effort and catch her wrist. With a rough shake, I make her drop it on the floor.

At the same time, the living room lights turn on, and Rachel stands behind me with her fingers over the light switch. "Found it."

The woman whose wrist I'm holding is the same one I saw the other day—Clock Dragon's girlfriend or wife.

"Mommy?" comes a child's voice.

A boy's head pops out through the crack of a half-open door and I jerk my head at Rachel to say, *Take care of the kid.*

"Hey, kiddo!" Rachel says, her voice heightening in pitch. "I'm so sorry if we scared you. We're friends of your mom's. Let's go back to your room and I'll show you some cool tricks, okay?"

Good thing I brought the witch.

The mother squirms and tries to punch me in the face with her other fist, but I catch it midair and squeeze until her knuckles crack.

"Tell your kid everything's fine," I say through clenched teeth.

"H-h-honey, it's okay." The mom says, a thick Latin accent rolling off her tongue. She forces a smile—an obvious twitch of the lip. "Go to your room, sweetheart, okay?"

The kid doesn't disappear just yet. Instead, he moves his head from side to side as Rachel approaches, trying to catch a glimpse of what's going on. He's either unsure about Rachel and me, or he doesn't understand why his mom's being so nice to him. I've been around a long time and have met my share of women like her. They're miserable with their lives, can't regulate their emotions, and take their shit out on their kids.

This woman is also pretty young. If I were to guess, I'd say anywhere between nineteen and twenty-five, which means her son probably wasn't part of her plan.

"Go!" she finally shouts, and the boy runs back into his room.

"He isn't immortal," I say.

She gives me a venomous look.

"What I mean is, he could die. Any day. He could get hit by a car... He could get leukemia."

Her sunken, hateful eyes turn on me.

"And here you are treating him like shit," I continue.

She tries to pull away, but when she realizes I'm not letting go, spits in my face. "What the fuck is your problem, you stupid *cabrona*? Don't you dare talk to me about my son. What do you want?"

"I need a word with your little boyfriend," I say.

She spits in my face again, the thick glob sliding

down onto my lips.

With my sleeve, I wipe it off. "You're a feisty one."

"Fuck you."

Although she isn't wearing any makeup, she's a natural beauty with long black curls, plush lips, and smooth olive skin. Her eyebrows are overplucked, but it somehow suits her face, as does the unsightly scar across her nostril. For pajamas, she's wearing a silk button-up top that caresses her unsupported breasts and silver pants to match. These clothes look to be the most expensive thing in this room.

"What's your name?" I ask.

"Miss nonayo fuckin' business," she says.

Without warning, I drag her across the kitchen and the moment she opens her mouth to shout out, I slap a hand over it. With my foot, I kick out one of her kitchen chairs, force her down, and point a stiff finger in her face.

"Not a peep."

She glares at me as I make my way over to her kitchen drawers. She could try to get up, maybe even attack me from behind, but I'll hear her before she even stands.

"What're you doing?" she asks.

Instead of answering her, I pull dish rags out from her bottom drawer—this seems to be a standard for a lot of people—and start wrapping her wrists and ankles.

"What're you doing?" she repeats, her voice an

octave higher.

Her anger is dissipating and being replaced by fear.

Good.

There's a good chance she underestimated my criminal abilities, being that I'm a woman. Now she knows I'm not here to fuck around. Or maybe I am. We'll see.

I crouch in front of her chair and bring my nose close to hers. "Where's your phone?"

She doesn't break eye contact.

"Where's your phone?" I repeat.

Nothing.

She's trying to protect her man, but at what cost? Her life? The life of her son? She has no idea who I am. Though if I were to guess, I'd say she doesn't think me capable of harming a child, especially after my insightful comment about the way she treats her son. Rachel being here isn't helping my case, either.

"Sweetheart," I say, smoothing my voice over. "I'm not here to hurt you or your boyfriend. All I'm asking for is a few minutes of his time."

No response.

Fuck it. I'm using my Lure. It washes over her like a drug swimming through her bloodstream.

She parts her lips, but nothing comes out.

Leaning forward to reveal some cleavage, I press my palms on her thighs, massaging her with my thumbs. Her eyelids flutter.

190

"You can trust me," I breathe. "I know you want to help me. In return, let me help you."

She's too worked up to say anything.

"You've never felt a woman's touch," I say, my voice soft.

She releases a staggered breath.

I smirk. "Where's your phone, beautiful?"

"It's... it's in the living room. B-b-beside the TV."

I stand up and brush the back of my hand along the side of her neck and along her ear. "Wait for me."

She nods fast with eyes sealed shut, and I disappear into the living room to get her phone. When I return, she's still breathing hard, squirming in her chair.

I crouch in front of her again, place the phone in front of her face, and it unlocks. Then, I scan through her messages.

It isn't hard to find her boyfriend—his name comes up as *Babe* with a red heart beside it. With my thumb, I scan through the messages, whipping out my speed-reading abilities.

Turns out Clock Dragon's name is Adrian, and her name is Camila.

I lean forward again, my hot breath against her face. "Oh, Camila," I say, and she rolls her head back. "Why don't you give Adrian a call? I'm sure he'd like to join us."

Still in a daze, she reaches for her phone and presses his name in her contact list as if her life depends on it.

"A-Adrian," she says, her voice husky. "You need to come home. No... Not the boys. Only you."

The sound at the other end is muffled—a deep, choppy voice.

I squeeze her thighs again.

"No... Right now," she says, her hypnotized eyes rolling up at me. Without saying goodbye, she ends the call, drops the phone on her lap, and fights to catch her breath.

"Good girl," I say.

CHAPTER 23

The moment the front door opens—a soft clicking sound—I step away from Camilla. She's so out of it you'd think I dosed her with something.

I move toward the kitchen counter, and pull out a cheese-encrusted knife. While I enjoy using my awesome new wrist blades, there's nothing more empowering than holding a knife by its handle.

In the distance, heavy boots storm through the house.

"Camila?"

"I'm... I'm in here," Camila says.

At the same time, I shove a dishtowel into her mouth and her eyes squint with pleasure. For the last twenty minutes, I've teased her in more ways than I'm certain anyone has ever teased her. A few minutes longer, and her heart might have stopped.

When Adrian enters the dimly lit kitchen, his eyes almost pop out of that big head of his. Without hesitating, he reaches behind his back to grab something, probably a gun tucked inside his pants.

"Ah, ah, ah," I say, twirling the knife in my fist.

And that's why I wanted the knife. Wrist blades aren't the same when it comes to intimidation.

His jaw muscles pop out and he looks like he's fantasizing about tearing me in half.

"You," he says. It comes out as more of an accusation than anything. "What the fuck do you want?"

"So, you recognize me," I say.

"What's it matter?" he growls. He takes a step toward me. "I swear to God, if you fuckin' hurt her–"

In a flash, I press the knife's tip into Camila's neck and she moans. He wrinkles his nose, likely confused as to how any of this could be turning her on.

"Oh, trust me... I wasn't hurting her. But if you take another step, she dies."

Raising his hands to his scruffy face, he takes a step back. Around his neck is a long gold chain, which hangs over his white, oversized T-shirt, making him look threatening despite his current predicament.

"What do you want?" he grits out.

Cutting to the chase, I say, "How much is Lucius paying you?"

He arches a thick black eyebrow. "The fuck you talkin' about?"

He's testing me, but it won't work. Digging the point of my knife into his girlfriend's neck, I bare my teeth at him. "You know exactly what I'm talking about."

Camila is still too high on my magic to give a crap about what we're discussing. She's still moaning, and every time the cold tip of my knife touches her skin, she squirms in her chair.

"Look, lady, I don't know who you are or what you think you're doin', but Lucius isn't the kinda guy you wanna get involved with."

Smirking, I scoop Camila's wavy hair back and let it hang over the chair's backrest. Me touching his girlfriend seems to upset him more than the knife at her throat. "I'm well aware of what Lucius is capable of. I'm not after Lucius. I'm after someone else. And I'm not here to hurt anyone, Adrian." He swallows hard at the sound of his name. "I'm here to make you a deal."

He sucks on his teeth and raises his chin. "What makes you think I wanna make a deal with you? You're pointin' a knife at my girl's throat."

"You have a gun behind your back. I'm simply taking precautions. Toss me your gun, and I'll put the knife down."

When he goes to reach for it, I add, "Nice and slow."

He moves as if powered by some slow-motion device and without breaking eye contact.

I throw my chin out at the small kitchen table, where he places the gun—a black Glock 19—and slides it toward me. With one hand, I pick it up, unload it, and sweep it off the table. "Have a seat."

He pulls out a chair, sits down, and slides closer to his girlfriend. "Hey, baby, it's okay. I'm right here."

"Don't bother," I say.

He glares up at me, dark shadows spreading across his cheekbones. "What'd you give her?"

"I didn't give her anything," I say. "At least, nothing in pill form."

"You fuckin' injected—" he starts.

"I didn't dose her with anything, *brah*. Calm your ass down."

He slams a clenched fist on the kitchen table, but Camila is way too out of it to even flinch. "Is this about Adam Shaw? I was only asked to collect some money he owed us that night. I ended up robbin' the guy instead, so everything's square. Lady, what do you want from us? I haven't gone to the police. I don't give a shit about the dead guy—"

"Settle down," I say nonchalantly. Though in reality, I am relieved to know I won't have to kill him after I get what I want. "This isn't about that. You have access to somewhere I need to be."

Slowly, he sits back in his chair, the wood of the backrest creaking behind him.

"You're obviously privy to information most Feeb—most humans aren't," I say.

He knows exactly what I'm talking about, but his girlfriend doesn't. I can tell by the way his eyes keep darting her way like he's trying to protect her from this life.

"She isn't paying attention," I say. "And I promise you she won't be involved in any of this."

While I don't make a habit of seducing someone without finishing the job, it does serve its purpose now and then. This tactic works better on women than it does on men, especially men who are prone to aggression—they often can't handle it and try to take me.

"So, what's this about?" he asks.

"All you need to know is that like you, I have a job to do, and that job involves Lucius's new lover, Veerka."

"That vampire chick?"

I nod.

He laughs, revealing teeth as white as baking soda toothpaste.

"Are you nuts? You got any idea how hard it is to get near her? No one gets near Lucius without there being a shitload of vampires in a room. So you can bet your ass you ain't gettin' anywhere near Veerka."

"You've seen her," I say, watching him.

"I mean, yeah. Once or twice. But she wasn't alone. Listen, I don't know how you think I can help, but I ain't getting' involved in your shit. If they ever find out—"

"No one's gonna find out," I say.

Typically, I wouldn't discuss the details of my mark with a feeble. But this guy is precisely that—a feeble. He isn't going to rat me out. If he did, he'd be putting himself and his entire family at risk for helping me in the first place. And if he's dumb enough to try to run to Lucius to tell him about my request, Lucius will wonder how I knew to go through Adrian for information, which will destroy Adrian's trustworthiness within the Vampire Mafia.

He either helps me, or he dies. Simple as that.

He must know it, too. Sighing, he says, "What do you need me to do?"

"I need a strand of her hair," I say, feeling like a nut job as the words come out.

He gawks at me. "A strand of hair? What the fuck—"

Raising a flat palm, I close my eyes. "You don't get to ask questions. That's my demand, and in exchange, I'll pay you."

"How much?" he asks.

Glancing around his kitchen—a room no larger than the size of a rich person's en suite bathroom—I realize this guy's desperate for money if he's working for the Vampire Mafia.

"Three thousand dollars," I say.

His laugh reverberates off his kitchen cabinetry.

Well, it was worth a shot.

"Bitch, are you insane?" he says, still laughing. "Three thousand dollars. The fuck you think I am? An idiot? What you're askin' me to do could get me killed. Like I said, if they sense me doin' anythin' fishy..."

"How much does Lucius pay you?" I ask.

He hesitates, no doubt weighing how dangerous it might be for him to talk about Lucius and his affairs. To speed up his thinking process, I shoot his girlfriend a look—one that says, *Don't make me hurt her.*

"I mean, it depends on the job," he says in a hurry. "And I just started workin' for him."

"Give me an average," I say.

He breathes out through his nostrils and looks at me as if to say, *Why bother? It's not like you can afford it.*

So I widen my eyes at his girlfriend again.

He sighs. "Twenty."

As I look into his honey-brown eyes, I think of little Pedro and I'm reminded of Jamal. Like Jamal, Pedro's future is dark and full of dangerous uncertainty. I'm betting Adrian started working for the Vampire Mafia to give his son a better life... To get the hell out of their neighborhood and build a life someplace safer. It's tough to make ends meet in a place where all you know is drugs, violence, and poverty.

The shitty part is that the vampires know this, especially ones like Lucius. That's why they prey on people who are desperate for money. And as it so happens, a lot of these people live in Estreenos.

Some days, when I'm riddled with guilt at the thought of Jamal's brutal murder, I try to imagine how long he would have survived the streets of Jormane had I not taken him in. When he turned five, his older brother was already teaching him how to use a gun.

Adrian gawks at me, likely wondering what the fuck's going on in my head.

Jamal could have ended up where you are, I think, staring back at him.

I can't help but wonder if Pedro will turn out like his father.

My throat tightens and I reach for a half-empty bottle of tequila sitting on their table.

Adrian arches a brow, probably thinking I've lost my mind. The moment the liquid burns my insides, my head clears and I'm reminded that I'm here for business. I could try to negotiate Adrian's payout, but I want this damn job done as soon as possible, and I'm not in the mood for the whole back-and-forth bullshit. And who knows? Maybe if I'm generous enough, he'll stop working for Lucius.

That is, if Lucius allows it.

"I'll give you a hundred," I say.

I realize I went high on my price, but the goal is to have him *want* to do the job, not resent me for it and somehow try to fuck it up for me. He also needs an incentive. What's stopping him from shooting me in the back as I leave this place? He'd be wasting his ammo, but that's not the point.

A crooked smile pulls at his face and he shakes his head like he doesn't believe me.

"What's so funny?" I ask.

This time, he stomps his boot and slaps his thigh

like I delivered a kickass joke.

In the distance, a small voice calls out, "Daddy?" and rapid footsteps come rushing down the dark hallway.

"Way to go," I say. "He heard you."

Adrian rushes to his son with open arms before the kid sees his mother tied up. "Hey, Pedro, my man."

Rachel comes chasing after Pedro but stops when she comes face-to-face with Adrian.

"It's fine, Rachel," I say, removing the mother's restraints. "We were just leaving."

Adrian plants a firm kiss on his son's cheek.

"Where's mamá?" Pedro asks.

Adrian brushes Pedro's hair away from his forehead. "Mommy's resting in the kitchen. I'll make sure she gets good sleep. Don't you worry, buddy."

The two of them disappear and a bedroom door closes. Seconds later, Adrian comes back empty-handed.

He flicks a light switch on, filling the living room with an ugly warm yellow light, and I wince like a vampire caught in the sun. Still standing next to the light switch, he spots Rachel, crosses his arms, and gives me an unimpressed look.

"Are you kidding me? You brought a kid with you?"

"I'm sixteen," Rachel says.

My eyelids go flat. "You work for the Vampire

Mafia. Who are you to judge? Hundred grand. Take it or leave it."

He won't be crazy enough to say no—he needs the money. And if he wants to provide a better life for his family, he'll do this job.

Finally, he lets out a long, defeated sigh.

"Whatever, lady. I'll get you your damn strand of hair. After you pay me, I don't want you showin' up here again. Ever. Is that clear? And if you don't pay me, you can bet your ass me and my boys will be comin' for you."

Fantasizing about my five-million-dollar check, I smirk. "Yep, you got it."

CHAPTER 24

Rachel plops herself down onto my living room sofa as if she owns it. "So... I'm still missing a vampire's toenail. And the strand of that chick's hair."

I fight the urge to smack her upside the head. "Are you kidding me? We were just talking to a guy who works with vampires. I'm getting you your damn strand. Why didn't you think to mention the toenail when we were there?"

She shrugs. "Oh, I don't know. Maybe because I was busy playing figurines with some random kid."

"Do you really need the nail?" I say through gritted teeth.

"Maybe not. We'll see. The hair is the most important part. It's how I'll set the locator spell."

"Good," I say. "Then figure it out without a toenail."

She sighs. "I mean, I've done it before, but the results aren't always precise. And I've never done it with a vampire before."

Across from us, Drax shakes his head, gets up, and slips into his Cheeto-stained hoodie. "I'm heading out. Either of you need anything?"

"Yeah," I say, my gaze fixated on Rachel. "How about some brain cells?"

Rachel glares back at me. "Didn't you say you're a demon?"

"Yeah," I say. "What's your point?"

"So, are you like, immortal?"

"What does this have to do with anything?" I ask, my voice rising.

"Well, you're fighting with a sixteen-year-old. And if you're immortal, you're probably like a gazillion years old, which makes you super immature for your age."

I turn my torso toward Drax, my arm resting against the sofa's back. "Can you also grab a bat?"

Without responding, he turns away and walks out.

Rachel gives me a dirty look before sticking her nose back into her spell book. It's about the size of a typical fiction novel and has all kinds of runes on the cover.

I'm not sure which version of Rachel annoys me more—the bubbly one I met at first or the bitchy one who looks at me like she wants to punch me in the throat.

"If you need a toenail for your portals, how'd you pull off getting into my apartment? It's not like I left any toenails behind."

She drops her book on her lap, which I assume is translation for, *You're such an idiot.*

Goddamn teenage hormones.

"It's different with vampires," she says. "You know... 'Cause they aren't alive."

I'm about to remind her that she wouldn't even know that vampires were real if it weren't for me, but instead, I keep my mouth shut and wait for her to continue.

She jabs her finger in the book as if I can read what it says. "It's right here. There's a whole section on tracking demons. I thought it was a bunch of hocus pocus stuff... But now that I know it's real, well, I'm gonna have to pay better attention to the actual spells."

"What do you mean?" I say. "You were winging it?"

She shrugs. "Kinda. My mom doesn't cook with a recipe book."

"Your mom's lasagna doesn't have the ability to blow up an entire city!"

She gradually raises her hands and inspects them with bewilderment. "Whoa. You think I have that kind of power? I mean... Not that I'd ever blow up a city. I'd never wanna hurt anyone. But... That's a lot of power."

"Don't get all power hungry on me," I say.

"I'm not," she retorts.

Rolling my eyes, I stretch out on my couch, punch the pillow under my neck, and call Mr. Mushroom up onto my lap. He jumps up so fast it's as if he was waiting for the invitation.

"You'd better get back home," I say, eyeing my retro clock. "Don't you have school or something?"

"Shit," she says. "Riskus, wake up!"

Her little goblin springs upright from behind the couch, his long silver hair resting in waves over his shoulders. He pulls it all back and ties it into a perfect little bun atop his head. Rachel then stands up, reaches into her pocket, and throws a purple powder at my wooden floor.

I'm about to scold her for adding more filth to this place when a huge opening tears through the air in front of me. Blue flame-like swirls move around the portal, and a gust of wind blows Rachel's auburn hair through the air.

"When is that guy giving you the strand?" she shouts over the loud noise.

"If all goes well, eight p.m. tonight," I say.

"What?" she shouts.

"Eight p.m.!" I shout back.

She nods. "I'll be back after school. I left my cell number on your coffee table."

And with that, she throws herself into the portal with her spell book clasped in her elbow and Riskus jumping in after her.

* * *

"That ain't how business works, lady," Adrian says.

Crossing my arms, I stare at him from behind the tip of my nose. "I don't give a shit about how you do your business. This is a different kind of business. The only way I'll know this hair belongs to

206

Veerka is if my plan works. And only when my plan works do you get paid."

He must think I'm crazy.

"I did the job," he says. "You owe me now."

"After," I say.

He tucks the strand of hair into a white envelope and slips it into his back pocket. Then, giving me an *I don't give a flying fuck who you think you are* look, he sucks on his front teeth and stares me down.

He's an arrogant little prick, and while it might be super easy for me to get what I want by using my Lure, or by kicking him in the balls, I'd rather intimidate him.

"You know vampires exist," I say matter-of-factly.

He doesn't seem too impressed with where I'm going with this.

"That must mean you know that magic exists."

He scoffs, saliva sprinkling onto my chin.

I'm not sure what I find more insulting—that the idea of magic makes him laugh or that I now have feeble juice on my face.

"I'm going to make myself very clear," I say, expanding my wings. At the same time, I extract my slick curved horns and lower my head to cast shadows under my eyes for dramatic effect.

All I'm missing now is a giant wind machine to creepily blow my hair back.

He steps back, his mouth a dark hole, but

nothing comes out.

At long last, a bit of fear.

"I only get paid once I complete my job, which means you only get paid if you did *your* job the right way. Now hand me the fucking hair before I gut you open and strangle you by your intestines."

He clears his throat, reaches into his back pocket, and hands me the envelope.

"Y-y-yeah, okay. Whatever, lady. Just take it."

Flipping the envelope around, I say, "Write down your cell."

He hesitates, as if giving me his phone number is equivalent to signing a contract with me. When I raise my eyebrows, he knows I'm not messing around. He pulls a pen out of his baggy pants, scribbles it down, and takes a step back.

Folding my wings, I snatch the envelope, force a smile, and tuck it into the pocket of my leather jacket. "Thanks. I'll be in touch soon. Now close your mouth. You look like a fucking moron."

CHAPTER 25

I'm about to enter The Orange Pub—I have plenty of time to waste until Rachel finishes school—when my phone vibrates in my jacket pocket.

It's Jamieson.

One thing's for certain—he's calling about Veerka. Flipping my phone open, I enter the bar anyways.

"What's up, Jamieson?"

"*What's up?*" he repeats. "Youngsters these days."

If only he knew how old I *really* was.

"I have some information for you," he continues. "The Lotus Hotel. That's where the party is going to be. Oh, and do you remember the smartphone you wanted, darling? Mr. Timothy is willing to meet you at his apartment on Third Street, apartment eight."

While to anyone else, that may have sounded like a harmless conversation about a new gadget, what Jamieson is telling me is *your mark will be at the Lotus Hotel at 8:00 p.m., room 308.*

"Oh, awesome," I say, feigning excitement. "I'll get ready and go pick up the phone."

"Enjoy it, darling."

His last word comes out playfully—his subtle way of reminding me that a shitload of money is on the line. Without responding, I hang up, walk toward the varnished mahogany bar counter, and sit on the very last bar stool.

Stephen the bartender—a young guy with a square face, an eyebrow with a sexy scar cutting through it, and seductive golden-brown eyes that make most barhopping girls swoon over him—reaches down by his waist and pulls out a bottle of Jack Daniel's.

"Three, or four?" he asks, trying to read me.

He knows me well.

"Five," I say, and he smirks.

He pulls out a frosted whiskey glass and without measuring, turns the bottle upside down, filling the glass up close to the brim. "How's that?"

I pick up the cool glass, raise it, and wink at him. "Perfect."

Before taking a sip, I inhale the scent and close my eyes. I enjoy inhaling the smell of alcohol as much as I do drinking it. Tilting the glass, I allow the liquid to touch my lips, almost teasingly. The burning satisfies me.

In only a few short hours, I'll be playing on my new Mac and scanning through real estate listings for a new place.

I smile at the thought and pour the entire glass of whiskey into my mouth.

At the same time, an older guy with a military baseball cap and a torn jacket pulls up a stool a few feet away from me. He sits down and grunts something at the bartender. When Stephen hands him a cold beer, the guy reaches for the pub's TV remote resting on the bar and aims it at the television.

The screen flickers a few times as he scans through the channels, skipping sports stations and infomercials. Finally, he lands on WTV News.

Barf.

Why would anyone want to ruin their buzz by watching the horrors of the world?

And while I want to ignore what's being broadcast, I can't.

A bold header scrolls across the television screen: Adam Shaw – No Foul Play Suspected.

News anchors start babbling about how the investigation is over and that the cause was that of *sudden death.*

Looks like the vampires got involved again. They tend to do this when a large investigation risks exposing the Underworld. I'm willing to bet that with all the creatures popping in and out of Adam's house in search of the talisman, Asmodeus put a stop to the feeble investigation.

"I'll have another," I say to Stephen, and he fills up my glass.

While no one else in this room knows it, I'm celebrating my freedom. I raise a glass at the television but lower it when a new headline pops up: Fire at Adam Shaw's House – Estimated Damages of 3.5 Million Dollars.

So that dumbass witch did burn it down.

Fucking idiot.

Whatever. I'm still celebrating.

Okay, maybe what I'm doing is trying to calm my nerves, which breaks my rule of not drinking on the job. Five million dollars is life-changing... if I pull this off. For the first time since working for Jamieson, I'm not entirely confident about this. I've barely taken the time to research my mark.

What the hell is wrong with me? I need to stop this self-sabotaging bullshit. It isn't hot.

"Excuse me," a man says. "Is someone sitting here?"

I wait a beat and turn to face the person responsible for interrupting my one-person party. He appears young, with smooth olive skin, but under his jet-black hair and along his temples are silver sideburns. They suit him, and I can imagine the ladies love the subtle gray. He smiles at me, revealing a set of perfectly straight teeth in the middle of his salt-and-pepper beard.

I can't help but wonder how much money he spent on his teeth and whether insurance covered it.

His eyes, two bright blue marbles under thick,

nicely trimmed brows, move toward the stool next to me as if trying to obtain an invitation.

Then, one eyelid droops lower than the other and he sways from side to side.

For a second there, I considered feeding off this hunk, but it's obvious he's hammered.

"Yeah, it's taken," I say, my voice monotone. "Meet Holly. My invisible friend."

He smirks, likely amused by my sense of humor. What he doesn't know is that I'm not trying to be funny—I'm trying to be a smart-ass instead of being an outright bitch. If he wants me to be a bitch, all he has to do is keep talking.

"You're funny," he says.

If I make my eyelids go any flatter, I'll be closing my eyes. So instead, I roll them and take a swig of my drink.

"Man, leave the girl alone," says an older guy sitting three stools down.

He readjusts his military baseball cap and glides his thumb across the condensation of his beer.

"Mind your business, old man."

And there it is—the egotistical prick living underneath a hot skin suit.

The guy with the baseball cap doesn't seem intimidated at all. He scoffs, points his beer at me, and says, "Is he givin' you a hard time? You don't deserve that, miss."

While I appreciate the concern and admire the chivalry, I can handle myself.

"I'm fine," I say, and the arrogant asshole next to me smiles as if he's won some arm-wrestling match.

Just as I go to take another sip of my drink, he pulls out the stool next to me, puffs out his chest like the testosterone-driven animal that he is, and sits down.

My right eyelid twitches.

Stephen, being the watchful bartender that he is, gives me a look that translates to *Want me to kick him out?*

I force a smile. "No need. Thanks, Stephen." I spin around on my stool and hop off. "You can put it on my tab."

"Where you going, gorgeous?"

Without looking at the drunk idiot, I brush past him and kick the bottom of his stool. His arms shoot up and he goes flying in the air before landing hard on his ass. The bar vibrates and the wooden floor planks shake.

The whole bar turns to look, but before anyone can say anything—and before Stephen can give me a hard time about keeping track of my bill without a credit card on file—I walk out of The Orange Pub on an angle, holding the wall to keep myself from falling.

Chapter 26

"So, let me get this straight," I say, staring at Rachel's red and black witchcraft book. "You can create a portal to Veerka's personal room at the hotel?"

Rachel looks up at me like I skipped most of high school. "No, that's not what I said."

I plop myself down onto my sofa and Mr. Mushroom jumps down before being squished like a pancake.

"Oh, I'm so sorry my little shnookums. Mommy didn't see—" I stop talking when I catch a glimpse of Rachel's judgmental gaze.

She jabs her finger into her book. "Like I already explained to you three times, this spell doesn't tell me where the person is or whether or not they're alone."

"So, get a better spell!"

She glares at me, then at my beer. It's my third one, and that's not counting the drinks I had at The Orange Pub, which is probably why I keep asking her to repeat herself. Placing it down on my coffee table, I sigh and reach for a water bottle.

Stop being a fucking idiot and sober up.

"This is the spell I've been practicing," she says. "It works well in the sense that it'll take you to who you're looking for... but there's no guarantee where you'll end up."

I scoff. "So you're telling me that if we time this wrong, I could end up appearing in front of a shitload of vampires."

She shrugs and I'm tempted to throw my water bottle at her head. I hate her nonchalant attitude—it's equivalent to saying, *Well, yeah, but that's not my problem, so I don't care.*

"You better hope your friend knows what he's talking about," she adds.

By friend, she means Jamieson the asshole.

He gave me a time—8:00 p.m., which doesn't tell me much. What that tells me is that Veerka's going to be at the hotel at that time. Jamieson has no idea what I'm planning. For all he knows, I'll do what I always do, and that's show up in some fancy evening gown and charm my way into Veerka's room.

Because of my lip ring microphone and pin camera, Jamieson knows how I work. He's made it clear that he doesn't understand how I'm so good at getting people to do what I want, but he doesn't seem to want to ask questions.

Tonight, however, it's important I leave my camera off until the right moment. If he sees me jumping into some magical portal, he'll either cut me out of his life completely, which means no more paychecks for me, or he'll yell at me until I go deaf.

"Even with the time he gave me," I say, "that doesn't tell me where she'll be inside the hotel. We need to find a way to—" I cut myself short when I hear Riskus snoring in Mr. Mushroom's bed.

"Your goblin," I say.

She frowns.

I wiggle a finger toward Mr. Mushroom's bed. "Your... thing."

"Thing?" she says, now glaring at me so intensely I fight the urge to tell her she might need glasses.

If she were a more experienced witch, I'd cover my eyes in fear of being transformed into some rodent. If looks could kill... well... never mind, that's a horrible example for an immortal to use.

"Whatever he is," I say. "I can't keep track of all the demon names out there."

She rolls her eyes and slaps her book. "He's a Serifus."

"Ser—" I try, but I'm too drunk to enunciate it. "Okay, yeah. Let's send him in."

She jolts upright, as does Riskus. "Send him in? Where? The hotel?"

Isn't it obvious? Where the hell else would I be sending him? The grocery store? I must be making a face. She leans back into the sofa and lets out a defeated sigh. Clearly, she doesn't want to do it, but at the same time, she wants what I promised her—the talisman and her grandmother's book.

"He's small enough to not be seen," I say. "I'd do this myself... go into her room early and wait for her, but vampires have crazy noses. I need to appear at the perfect moment if I don't want this tying back to me. All I need is for him to sneak into the vents or something and let me know when she's alone."

I could fly up onto the roof myself, but that would be suicide. If Veerka is going to be at the hotel tonight, that means Lucius will also be there, which means he'll have vampires everywhere.

This needs to be a quick in-and-out.

Riskus looks up at her like the loyal companion he is.

"Think you can do that?" Rachel asks.

He nods, his pointed nose wiggling on his face.

Realizing something, I ask, "How'd you send him into Adam's basement last time? It's not like you had any specific ingredients to take you there."

She points at one of her spell books. "The exact instructions were in the book. You know, the one you couldn't read."

"I can read just fine—" I argue, but she cuts me off.

"It wasn't a typical portal spell. It was specific to locating the talisman."

"Stupid magic," I say, and she looks at me like I unburied her dead grandmother. "Would you relax? You're so goddamn sensitive. You're sixteen, for fuck's sake. Grow up."

Pouting, she reaches for her lime-green rain jacket.

"Where're you going?" I ask.

Have I crossed a line? Sure, I need her help, but she needs me too if she wants her stuff back. What was I supposed to do? She's acting like a goddamn hormonal teenager—

Closing my eyes, I draw in a long, calculated breath.

That's exactly what she is... a teenager, and I'm being a drunken bitch.

I have to at least try to be understanding that she's a human pumped full of hormones. Maybe there's a reason she is the way she is. I have no intention of trying to figure it out, but I can cut back on my bitchiness.

"Look, I'm sorry," I say, not quite meaning it. "I want this to be over, okay?"

"Yeah," she says, her voice now monotone. "Me, too. Come on, Riskus."

Rising to my feet, I clench my water bottle, causing it to crack in half and spill on my feet. "Where are you going?"

She throws an oversized baseball cap over Riskus's head and wraps a child's jacket around him. "To get this over with so I can move on with my life. We should get Riskus inside before the party starts. Are you staying here, or are you coming to do your job? The least you could do is call me a taxi."

I'm about to point her toward my closet and tell her to find herself a broom, but I stop myself before the words come out. I reach down into my pile of many leather jackets and grab the first thing my fingers find. Slipping it on, I say, "All right, let's go. And there are tons of taxis outside."

Rachel and Riskus walk ahead of me, resembling a mother and her child. Something looks off, but I doubt anyone in San Halos will take the time to look at them twice. It's funny to see Riskus walk like a penguin with his long, oversized Converse sneakers, but it's better that than his hideous demon feet.

How does she keep him a secret, anyway? Does she typically avoid walking with him in daylight? I'm certain his appearance is much different in the eyes of a feeble.

As we walk out into the streets of downtown San Halos, Riskus runs his fingers along my new Ducati bike.

"Hey!" I hiss, and he retreats like he touched a pot of boiling water.

"Is that yours?" Rachel asks.

"Apparently," I say.

A hint of a smile appears on her face. "It's nice."

I'm too stunned by her compliment to respond. So instead, I wave an arm up at the nearest yellow taxi I can see and the driver comes speeding toward us as if his life depends on it. His tires screech as he slams his breaks and Riskus jumps back. Behind him, another taxi driver wails on his horn.

This isn't unusual in San Halos—everyone's in a rush, everyone's bitchy, and everyone is looking to make a fast penny. This city reminds me a lot of New York City, only with way more shadow dwellers.

The first taxi driver flips him the bird, but his competitor keeps honking like a psychopath, arms flailing above his head.

What the fuck does he think will happen? That we'll ask *him*, the maniac flipping out in his car, to give us a lift?

"Get inside," I say, opening the first taxi's back door.

Rachel rounds her back to get in, while Riskus simply hops in.

Standing up straight, I make my way over to the aggressive taxi driver. When he sees me approaching, an exaggerated smile morphs his face, and he sticks his head out the window.

"Hey, pretty lady," he says. "I didn't mean to startle you and your daughter."

My *daughter*? He's digging his own grave.

"John and I go way back. He poaches my clients, ya know? How 'bout you hop on in here and I'll take good care of—"

I don't even give him the time to finish. I'm still buzzed from my day drinking, irritated by Rachel's maddening teenage attitude, and stressed out about having to kill an untouchable vampire tonight. The last thing I need is some fucking asshole blaring his horn in my ear.

With both hands, I grab his front bumper and raise the front of his car until I can see the underneath.

"Hey! Hey! What the fuck, lady? What the fuck are you doing? Jesus Christ!"

Stepping back, I let go of his car, and it comes slamming down on the ground. His suspension falls apart and his tires blow—a sound so satisfying it's almost equivalent to the feeling of cold liquor sliding into my stomach.

His car's alarm goes off and the driver jumps out in a panic. Pushing him aside, I reach inside his taxi and tear out his dashcam. The last thing I need is for this video to go viral. Fortunately, no one has a phone's camera pointed at me, and before giving anyone the time to change that, I climb into our taxi with the other guy's busted dashcam in my fist.

Our driver looks at me with bulging eyes and a line of drool on his chin.

"What?" I say. "I'm a powerlifting champion. Now come on, we don't have all day. Take us to the Lotus Hotel."

CHAPTER 27

"Holy shit," I say. "What is he? A monkey?"

Rachel doesn't respond and instead leans the weight of her body against the green dumpster behind her.

Before I have time to blink again, Riskus has made his way up the brick wall at the back of the Lotus Hotel.

"So is he going in through the roof?" I ask. "And how will he know who Veerka is?"

I tried to discuss all of this before we went ahead with the mission, but Riskus went running off like a kid at a waterpark.

"Riskus is smart," she says. "He'll figure it out."

Arching an eyebrow, I wait for her to explain to me how he's going to communicate to us that he's found her.

"We have a telepathic connection," she says.

I'm about to start laughing when I realize we live in a world full of magic. So instead, I keep my mouth shut, something that doesn't come easily to me.

We stand in silence, intoxicated by the

alleyway's garbage fumes. In downtown San Halos, it doesn't matter how fancy an establishment is; there are alleyways everywhere and they're typically filled with garbage, piss, and vampires.

Staring at the back of the Lotus Hotel, I breathe out and glance down at my phone.

7:21 p.m.

Goddamn it. I don't have the patience to sit here for another forty minutes. I'm about to start walking down the alley when Rachel snorts and says, "Seriously?"

I spin around. "Seriously, *what*?"

"You're going to a bar, aren't you?"

I shrug at her like the answer's obvious. Where else would I be going?

"Are you that miserable with your life that you have to drink every damn day?"

Who does she think she is? She knows nothing about me. And the last thing I'm going to do is listen to some sixteen-year-old's bullshit about—

"Look, I get it," she says. "My dad's ex-military."

I stop talking. Where is she going with this?

"Ever since he came back from some mission in Russia, he hasn't been the same. Like, at all. He's angry all the time."

She averts her gaze and kicks at the cracked asphalt under her feet.

Is this where I'm supposed to step in and comfort her? It isn't my strong suit, so instead, I stand there staring at her, waiting for her to finish talking.

"He drinks every night until I don't even recognize him anymore. Mom tries to defend him by saying he's been through a lot, even when he gets physical. I'm sure he's been through hell, but that doesn't give him any right to treat us like shit or put his hands on my mom. We're the ones suffering now because of it. Grandma would have turned him into a frog if she were still here..."

Is that why Rachel is so snippy with me all the time? Because my drinking reminds her of her abusive father?

"I... I'm sorry," I say.

I'm not sure how else to respond. The kid's hurting badly, and while I may be cold most of the time, I don't enjoy seeing a young girl suffer at the hands of her father. I especially don't like the idea of hurting someone because I can't control my anger without numbing myself. It's selfish, and it makes me feel worthless. I know I'm better than that. So instead of giving in to my craving for alcohol, I make my way back to her, lean against the garbage dumpster's cool metal, and aim my face toward the sky.

"Don't tell Drax," I say.

"Tell him what?"

"That you stopped me from going to a bar. He's never been able to."

After a prolonged silence, I say, "So, you think your little minion's gonna pull this off?"

Without blinking, she says, "He will."

"How long have you had him?"

She shakes her head. "You make him sound like a pet."

"Isn't he?"

"No," she says sternly. "He's family."

I'm about to say, *I consider Mr. Mushroom family, but he's still my pet,* but refrain from doing so.

Sighing, I check my phone again.

7:26

Jesus Christ.

Fidgeting, I shift the weight of my body onto one leg. There's too much time to kill, and I'm not a patient person.

Rachel must notice my discomfort. She turns toward me, gives me a look full of attitude, and says, "How old are you?"

"Excuse me?"

"How old are you?" she repeats.

I scoff. "How is that any of your business?"

"Vampires can be super old, so I'm wondering if you are, too," she says. "When were you born?"

"First of all," I say, "I'm not a vampire."

"Answer the question," she says.

Sighing, I kick a pile of pebbles away from me. "October twenty-seventh, one thousand and eighteen."

"So you're a Scorpio," she points out.

"Really?" I say. "I'm over a thousand years old

and the first thing you point out is my zodiac sign?”

Smirking, she says, “I’m an Aries.”

“Big surprise.”

She frowns. “What’s that supposed to mean?”

I resist the urge to laugh at the ugly face she’s making. “Always wanting to be the center of attention.”

“Better than being a coldhearted stuck-up bitch,” she says.

For the first time since meeting this girl, I’m speechless. I’m running as many comebacks as I can through my mind, but I’m coming up blank. She isn’t wrong.

“Well...” I say, “at least I get paid to be this way.”

She scoffs and turns away. At the same time, Riskus comes running from across the street with a clenched fist by his head. He grins from ear to ear, waddling with every step.

“What is it, Riskus?” Rachel asks.

Saying nothing, he reaches his fist into the air and drops a torn piece of clothing into Rachel’s palm. Is this Veerka’s? If so, what’s this for? Accuracy? It must be. Rachel never did get her toenail, so maybe some of Veerka’s clothing, along with her hair, will help her create the perfect portal. I’m happy to know she won’t be sending me somewhere stupid, like between two sheets of drywall.

“Still nothing?” Rachel asks.

Riskus nods fast. “She is early. But she is not

alone. Not safe yet."

"Okay," Rachel says, patting Riskus on the head. He seems to like this. His grin widens and his eyes turn into vertical lines. "Let us know when she's alone, okay?"

He nods again and disappears as fast as a squirrel on speed.

"You feel confident about your portal?" I ask.

She crosses her arms, refusing to look at me.

"Listen," I say, "I'm sorry I stole from you. I shouldn't have done that. But you don't understand. You're only a—"

Swinging around so fast her hair sweeps the air beside her, she aims a finger at me. "Don't even say it. I'm so sick of hearing that. I'm not a kid. I'm legally an adult in two years."

"When this is over," I say, "I'll give you back your shit and you can go home and pretend none of this ever happened, okay?"

She doesn't respond, so I figure that means she agrees with my terms.

I press my back against the dumpster and lower myself to the ground. For some reason, I suspect we'll be here longer than expected.

"You say when *this* is over," she says. "What does that mean, anyway? What is it you have to do?"

I roll my head against the dumpster to look at her. "My work is confidential." I don't want to tell her she's too young to know what I do. Even if she weren't too young, it's not like I go around telling people I'm a hitwoman. She already knows I'm a demon, which is way more than what most people know. "So don't worry about what I do and trust me when I say I'll give you back your stuff. You have my word. Okay?"

CHAPTER 28

"Get up!" Rachel says.

"Wh-what?" I say, rubbing my eyes.

Ogre balls. Did I fall asleep? What time is it?

"She's alone," Rachel hisses. Then, she steps back, pulls a pouch out of her pocket, and starts talking gibberish.

It's hard not to laugh at her because it sounds like she's making up words. But judging by the pink and purple light coming out of the tips of her wand, it's obvious she isn't making shit up. She's casting some sort of spell, and I'm assuming it's for my portal.

She shouts one more thing, then throws a handful of powdery white dust in the air. At once, the air in front of her spins as if swirling around the blades of a blender.

"Go, now!" she says.

I hesitate. I want to trust her, but the truth is, she doesn't trust me, which makes this entire partnership a bit risky. But if she wants her stuff back—and I know she does—she'll make sure I succeed in doing what I have to do.

Holding my breath, I lunge straight into the portal.

There's a loud ringing in my ears, and for a second, I feel like I just stepped off the world's fastest rollercoaster. But the next thing I know, I'm lying flat on my face on what feels like a bearskin rug.

I'm all for killing sick sons of bitches, but using an animal's carcass for decoration? Not my thing. Repulsed, I push myself up and crawl onto my knees.

"I didn't realize I was receiving company," comes a cold voice.

What the fuck?

I know that voice.

And why couldn't I have landed on my feet?

Slowly, I look up to find her sitting on her bed, her perfectly toned legs crossed under a silk red dress. Her hair, long and ash blond, rests over her shoulder and drapes down over her chest. Her skin is so white she looks like she's been dipped inside a giant bucket of white latex paint.

"Holy mother of—" I breathe.

"What's wrong, Emily?" she says. "You look like you've seen a ghost."

I part my lips, but nothing comes out. So instead, I blink hard to make sure I'm not hallucinating.

How is this even possible?

I thought she was dead.

This isn't possible… Rachel must have sent me back in time.

"What's the matter, Emily?" she says. "Cat got your tongue?"

The words come out of her mouth with a seductive hiss.

"Elizabeth," I breathe.

It isn't her vampiric charm that's throwing me off my game; it's that I know this woman. Elizabeth—Veerka, now—and I were lovers centuries ago.

"I thought you were dead," I say.

She throws her head back and releases a playful chuckle. "Oh, Emily—"

"It's Alexis now."

Her smirk doesn't falter. "Alexis. Interesting."

I stand up and dust my pants off. "What kind of name is Veerka?"

With an elevated chin, she watches me, and I can't help but be drawn to her.

Elizab—Veerka, is the only person who could make me weak in the knees. And when I knew her all those years ago, she was a feeble.

"Why are you here, Emily?" she asks.

Every time she calls me by my old name, it brings me back hundreds of years ago. I don't like to look back—I'm more of a live-in-the-moment kind of gal.

"Alexis," I correct again.

She flicks her wrist, uncrosses her legs as if purposely trying to make me look up her dress, then crosses them again.

"Well..." she draws a circle on her bedsheets. "That's going to take some getting used to."

Five million dollars. Five million dollars. Five million dollars.

Extracting my wrist blades, I lower my head and clench my fists. This woman isn't Elizabeth anymore. She isn't the woman I loved. That woman died a long time ago, and this shell of an existence is messing with my head.

"You don't seriously plan on killing me, do you, darling?"

Unlike me, she still has her British accent, which makes everything that much harder. Her cheekbones, high and defined, give her a domineering look that I wouldn't normally find attractive. But on her, it does something to me. Her bright blue eyes dart back and forth between me and my blades.

Why isn't she afraid? Is she *that* powerful? Could she kill me if she wanted to?

The only reason I'm able to even consider killing her is that she's already dead.

Leisurely, she stands on her high-heeled shoes, the clicking sound hypnotizing me as she approaches.

I want to slash her throat, but I can't. In fact, I can't move at all.

"Oh, my sweet Emily," she says, gliding a finger down my arm. "If you're here to kill me, it's because someone's sent you. Who sent you, Emily?"

She stares into me and my mouth goes dry.

Snap the fuck out of it, Alexis.

"It doesn't matter," I say.

She leans in close, her lips almost touching mine, and moves toward my ear.

"I think it matters," she whispers. "You don't want to kill me, love."

She's right—I don't.

But for five million big ones, I will.

Besides, she's gone all evil now and she's causing a bunch of problems in the city. I can't let my personal centuries-old feelings get in the way of that.

"What if I had a way to give you what you wanted?" she says.

She's a vampire. I can't trust a word she says. She must sense my reluctance; she giggles the way I remember and plays with the tips of her long hair.

"I'm not an idiot, Emily," she says. "I know many want me dead. I've angered quite a few people in this city. Rumor has it that I'm after Asmodeus's throne."

"Are you?" I ask.

A twinkle flashes in her eyes, but she doesn't say anything. I know that look, and it confirms the rumors.

"You would think after so many years... gender

inequality would no longer be an issue," she says.

I grimace at her. "What're you talking about?"

"Asmodeus," she says plainly. "He's old-school. He also happens to be a walking corpse. It's time for him to retire, Emily, don't you think?"

I'm about to open my mouth when she glides a finger across my collarbone and down my chest. As much as I want to slap her hand away, I can't. Instead, I take in her sexy figure and fantasize about having my way with her.

"You know how this goes, Emily. A woman tries to take power and every man in the city tries to take her down."

"I'm not sure that's what this is about."

Her finger moves upward and over my lips. "I don't know what you've been told, love, but I'm not the enemy."

How can I believe her? I realize Jamieson isn't the nicest guy around, and I don't know *why* he wants her dead so badly, but I do what I do for the money—I don't do it to help people. And right now, Veerka's old ties to me are getting in the way of me and my riches.

"Why don't you join me?"

I almost laugh in her face. "Join you?"

I take in her pale shoulders, her perky breasts, and her flawless hips. God, what I wouldn't do to have my way with her.

The problem with Veerka and me is that we were never able to have each other—at least not physically. Back then, I wasn't able to control my powers, and I'd often end up killing anyone I had sex with. I loved this woman... truly loved her. And yet, I could never have her. It was always a game of cat and mouse between the two of us.

I spent years trying to control my power, killing countless people in the process to have her. I'm not proud of my approach, but that's how badly I wanted her to be mine.

"I'm a vampire now, Alexis."

Finally, she uses my new name. I'm about to thank her for stating the obvious when she bites her lower lip and scans me from head to toe. "Do you have any idea how long I've been waiting for you?"

Is she toying with me? For all I know, she'll try to kill me the moment I put my guard down. This is exactly why I avoid emotion—it gets in the way of shit.

She takes a step closer, and I stand still, unable to look away from her piercing eyes. Slowly, she wraps her fingers around my wrist and tickles my skin with her long red-painted nails. But then, out of nowhere, she applies more pressure into my forearm, puncturing my skin.

I yank away, but she holds me tightly.

"Relax," she breathes.

As dark blood slips out of my cut, she bows her head and glances up at me with a sexy smirk. She parts her lips, her cool breath landing on my arm, and sinks her teeth into me. The pain sends a hot, throbbing sensation between my legs.

I don't stop her. Instead, I let her drink, my eyes fluttering as I imagine myself tearing off her clothes.

Veerka knows I can't feed off vampires, and she also knows vampires can't turn me into one of them. She saw it for herself over seven hundred years ago in York, England. I can't remember the exact date, but I remember her eyes.

* * *

"Emily," Elizabeth hissed.

She lifted her long taupe cape and hurried across the cobblestones. Her flawless face was hidden within the shadow of her hood, illuminated partially by a pair of sconces hanging above a door in the alleyway.

Unable to stop staring at her, I smiled.

God, she's beautiful, I thought.

There was a certain innocence to her that made me want to caress her, protect her, and ravage her all at the same time.

Invigorated by the idea of roaming the city's most dangerous street at such a time, Elizabeth covered her mouth and released an anxious giggle. Peasant feebles never ventured to this place at night, but I knew Elizabeth wanted excitement, so that night, I decided to offer it to her.

The alley was quiet, aside from loud drunken voices coming from behind closed doors.

We were about halfway down the alley when out from the shadows came an overly tall vampire in pointed shoes, a bloodstained white tunic, and torn suede pants. As he moved toward us, an evil smile deformed his pasty face. With a bowed head, he dragged his claws against the alley's stone walls, a loud scraping noise filling the air around us.

Dry blood sat on his chin, and his fangs looked like they were throbbing for more.

"Ladies," he said, soothingly.

Admittedly, he used a different word, but I'm not going to bother trying to remember Middle English terms.

"You should not be traveling such roads at night," he said.

Elizabeth gasped, and the vampire's attention instantly shifted toward her. Pointing his nose at the starlit sky, he sniffed like a bloodhound, his rust-colored smile cracking even wider.

When he caught my scent, however, he winced.

"What's the matter?" I asked. "Not what you're hungry for?"

This was it... my chance to show Elizabeth how badass—

The next thing I knew, searing pain penetrated my neck and I was floating in the air with the vampire's mouth wrapped around my throat. Pulling his fangs out, he dropped me to the ground as if I were nothing more than a bag of garbage.

What the fuck? How had he moved so fast?

Wiping his thin bloody lip, he hissed at the night sky.

I shot back up, fists clenched. "That all you got, *motherfucker*?"

Okay, what I did call him was a *smell-feast*, but *motherfucker* sounded way more intense.

He must have realized that biting into me was pointless. In a split second, his hungry eyes turned on Elizabeth. She looked petrified. Stepping backward, she tripped over her cloak but caught herself against the wall before tumbling over.

That's when I lost my shit.

Without thinking, I grabbed the good-for-nothing vampire by the jaw, his lower canines puncturing holes in my fingers, and I pulled down as hard as I could. He shrieked, the sound causing my ears to ache, and reached for his dislocated jaw that hung awkwardly in front of his neck.

With a tight fist, I punched him in the nose—an unnecessary attack, but one that felt good, nonetheless. He stumbled backward as dark blood poured out of his nostrils, resembling black paint across a blank canvas.

I reached inside my cloak, extracted my hand-carved stake, and spun it twice in my palm before stabbing him through the heart.

A wave of panic washed over him, but within seconds, he erupted into a pile of ash. The brown and gray specks floated through the damp air before landing on the cobblestones at our feet.

When I turned to Elizabeth, she looked mortified.

"That... that was far too close," she said.

I felt stupid for how quickly everything got out of hand. Never once had I seen a vampire move so fast before. I couldn't even anticipate his attack. What if he'd attacked her first? He could have killed her.

"Way too close," I said.

The corner of her lip suddenly pointed upward. Why was she smiling?

"How is any of this funny?" I asked.

"I'm not laughing," she said, her focus lingering on my lips.

I should have been freaking out about what happened, but I was too busy staring at her body to care.

She wanted me... it was obvious.

Without warning, I pinned her hard against one of the alleyway's doors and she breathed out excitedly. Holding her down, I kissed her lips, her neck, her chest.

My kissing evolved into aggressive sucking until at last, she pulled her cloak out of the way, raised her dress, and reached inside her undergarment, pleasuring herself.

It was torturous. I wanted to be the one to touch her, but I couldn't. It was too much of a risk.

So instead, I held her by the throat as her movements quickened, and I imagined myself being the one to pleasure her. As her exhilaration amplified, I pressed my body against hers and thrust, our bodies moving as one.

It wasn't what I wanted, but it made me feel something... I felt close to her.

Then, she did something I couldn't have anticipated; she reached for the bite wound on my neck and spread the blood across my throat, my chin, my mouth... and kissed me hard.

I'd be lying if I said it didn't excite me.

She forced her tongue inside my mouth, filling it with the taste of warm blood until at once, her body contracted and a shrill whimper jumped from her mouth and into mine.

To stop myself from doing something I might regret, I dug my nails into the wooden door behind her and counted to three.

When it was over, her body relaxed and she stood silently with her lips covered in blood and her cheeks a hot pink. I kissed her over and over again, feeling like I'd ingested a lethal amount of drugs.

Every time we did this, the torture of it led me to believe I might die. But there was one problem: the idea of not having her at all made me *want* to die.

CHAPTER 29

"It isn't complicated," Veerka says. "You stage my death and we both win."

I scoff. She makes it sound like it's as easy as cracking an egg.

She must sense my reluctance. Tilting her head to the side, she smiles. God, I've missed this woman. But... is she truly the same person I once knew? She can't be. A few hundred years changes a person. What if this is a setup?

What throws me off my game is how when I look into those bright blue eyes of her, I can't help but feel at home. As cheesy as it might sound, it's like our souls are connected. It's always felt that way with her.

"How does your boss like to receive confirmation?" she asks.

"Depends on the job. Sometimes before, and always after."

"So not the act of killing itself?" she says.

She can't possibly think I'm that stupid. "I'm not giving him anything to use against me, so no, I don't record me killing someone. I show him the mark, and then the body."

"Well, that's simply ridiculous. How does he expect you to kill a vampire and prove it?"

"I don't know," I say, getting impatient. "He's never asked me to before. Anyways, he trusts me."

She tightens her lips, looking bemused. "Trusts you?"

"I may have my faults," I say, "but when it comes to work, I do my job."

I'm about to make some smart-ass remark about how she wouldn't understand that because she probably never worked a day in her life, when something bright catches my eye.

"Where'd you get that?" I ask, pointing at the huge shiny stone around her neck.

She reaches for it. "This old thing? Lucius gave it to me."

Of course.

"Buying your love?" I ask, gritting my teeth.

If there's one thing that irks me more than Veerka now being a vampire, it's the idea of another person, or thing, touching her. No matter how much time has passed, I still think of her as mine. Whether that's a succubus thing or a Scorpio thing... I'm not sure.

"He tries," she says casually.

"You don't love him?" I ask.

What the fuck is wrong with me? I haven't felt jealousy in centuries.

244

"He's a stepping-stone," she says.

She keeps looking up at the ceiling—one hell of a fancy ceiling, might I add—almost as if annoyed by the very thought of him. Does she not care about him? Is she using him? One reason I fell in love with Veerka way back when was her innocence, but I suspect she lost that a long time ago.

Turning away from me, she leans against her bedpost. "He underestimates me."

I know Veerka. I don't give a shit if I haven't seen her in centuries. I know who she is deep down. And deep down, she's a soft soul—a good person. Her life has no doubt toughened her up, but she's always been inherently sensitive. Could becoming a vampire have stripped that away from her? When she says that he underestimates her, I wonder: is that *exactly* what she wants? Is she playing him? Is she using her sensitive side to toy with his mind? By now, she must have realized how valuable her innocence can be—or at least, what's left of it.

What do I know? Maybe everything about her is a lie, and she *has* become a monster.

I must be glaring at her because she lets out an entertained laugh. "Oh, Alexis. Do you honestly think I could ever love such a man? He's like Asmodeus. All he wants is power."

"Like you," I say.

She doesn't deny it. "Perhaps. But at the end of the day, I want what's best for everyone."

Bullshit. No vampire wants what's best for

everyone.

"And what's that?" I ask.

"A life without fear of retribution."

So Kyle the rock man was right. Veerka's trying to bring shadow dwellers and feebles together.

"You think feebles and shadow dwellers can coexist," I say matter-of-factly.

Of all people, she should know that such a thing isn't possible. It never has been, and if she thinks being a vampire for a few years, maybe even a century, makes her capable of changing that, she's delusional.

"It's better than the alternative, isn't it?" she says.

I gawk at her. "And what would that be?"

"Oh, Alexis. You know exactly what's going on. Lucius and Asmodeus want to control feebles. They're allowing humans to pay fortunes to become vampires. Do you have any idea what that's going to cause? Vampires will outnumber feebles, and eventually, feebles will become extinct. Either that, or they'll continue to be farmed and kept in torturous living conditions for the sole purpose of feeding us."

What the hell does she care? She's a vampire. Why would she give two shits about feebles?

I must be making a face. Deliberately, she walks toward me again and plays with the front of my shirt.

"How can vampires survive without food?" she

says.

I knew this was really about her needs.

"Lucius is old-school, Alexis, same as Asmodeus. The only thing they care about is power, money, and blood. Lucius assures me that there are plenty of feebles to go around, but he doesn't look ahead, the way I do. What this world needs is the mind of a woman—"

"You mean your mind," I cut her off.

She smirks. "Alexis, think about it. Eventually, Asmodeus and his vampire leaders will lose control. More and more vampires will stop obeying their commands, and they'll feed off of innocent feebles. Some may even turn their entire families into vampires simply for immortality."

While I hate to admit it, she's right. Things could get ugly pretty fast if vampires start to overpopulate.

"What do you say?" she says. "Won't you join me?"

No, I won't, you psychotic bitch.

She stands so close to me that her breasts almost press against mine, and I hold my breath. All I want to do is throw her onto that massive bed behind her, pull up her dress, and have my way with her.

"Be my partner," she says.

Partner? What kind of partner are we talking about? The corner of her lip pulls up, revealing a sharp vampire fang, and it becomes apparent to me that this partnership is going to involve a lot more than business.

"How can I be your partner?" I ask. "You're working alongside Lucius."

"For now," she says. "But with your help, we can change that."

When I don't respond, she leans in close, her cool breath slipping past my lips. "What do you say, darling?"

It takes all my willpower not to press my lips against hers. Although everything inside of me is screaming to run the other way, I can't. I've wanted Veerka most of my life, and now I'm being offered that chance. I'm also being given an opportunity to take down two vampires I despise more than Hades.

"What's in it for me?"

Aside from getting to fuck you, I mean.

My boldness seems to intrigue her. "I'll pay you."

"How much?"

"I'll pay you whatever your boss pays you."

"You're asking me to cross my boss. Not only will I lose my job, but I'll have a target on my back."

"I'll give you double what he pays you."

I pause, mulling it over. "Triple it and you have yourself a deal. But if you so much as try anything—"

She leans in, grazing her lips against mine.

"I believe we'll make a wonderful team, Alexis." She runs her nails across my left cheek and I wince.

Without warning, she presses her cold lips against mine. I don't pull away. Instead, I breathe out hard and grab her by the waist, prepared to do to her what I couldn't all those years ago.

But as I push her back, she grabs me by the throat.

Holy shit she's strong.

I like it.

It makes me want her even more.

"Not yet," she says with a sly smirk. "First, you have to kill me."

CHAPTER 30

"Do you have any idea how hard it was to get this close?" I say through my lip ring microphone. I point my wireless pin camera through Veerka's window.

Inside her hotel room, she sits in front of her vanity. Staring at her reflection—or at least, pretending to—she applies bright red lipstick.

"That's her," Jamieson responds into my earpiece.

It's almost like he didn't believe I could get this close. I'm guessing that's why the payout is so high.

"How did you get up there—" he starts.

"You know how this works," I cut him off.

He knows exactly how this works. I do my job, and he doesn't question me about it. This is why I get paid the big bucks while he sits behind his fancy desk. I'm the pro and he knows it, and he also knows better than to ask me questions about my abilities.

He clears his throat. "Are you sure she's alone?"

"I'm sure," I say. "Lucius left a few minutes ago.

I overheard him saying he'll be back shortly."

"Good, good..." he says.

As planned, Veerka gets up and turns around until her stone necklace comes into view. It's an oval-shaped blue sapphire that sits in a white gold encasing.

I aim the camera at Veerka's neck and Jamieson lets out a sharp breath.

"The Eye of Poseidon," he breathes.

The way he mentioned the necklace leads me to believe it's something powerful, but I don't care. The whole point of him seeing it is so he can associate Veerka's physical form with the pile of ashes I plan on showing him afterward.

He might try to get me to take it, but too bad. Veerka won't actually be dead, which means it'll still belong to her.

"Listen, I have to make this fast," I say. "Wanted you to confirm the mark."

He clears his throat again, probably trying to figure out how to smooth talk his way into getting that necklace. But I don't give him the time.

"I'll reconnect as soon as the job is done."

And with that, I turn off my equipment. A little beep in my ear confirms that everything's been shut down. I knock on Veerka's window with my fist—an agreed-upon signal that lets her know I'm ready.

She opens her mouth and calls out a name— Traveeno.

Her room door gradually opens and a vampire with long, wavy blond hair and a snug tuxedo steps in. Seemingly afraid of her, he doesn't make eye contact.

It would appear she's more powerful than I gave her credit for.

She tells him to come in and closes the door behind him. The moment they're close to each other, she reaches for his face in a flirtatious manner, and it takes everything in me not to smash her window into a thousand pieces.

I know nothing's going to happen—this is all part of the plan—but I can't help my jealousy. I don't want her touching anyone else. She inches closer and closer, pressing her body against his, and he stands there like a statue.

Without warning, Veerka slices his throat with her nails and he gasps, reaching for his neck. She takes another swing, this time tearing through his spinal cord and muscle tissue until his head falls backward. It hangs against his upper back, holding on by only a thin piece of white skin until finally, the skin snaps and his head smashes on the floor.

With a proud smile, Veerka licks her fingers, then pokes the vampire in the chest to tip him back. His body goes down like a domino but explodes into a cloud of dust before hitting the ground.

That's my cue.

I open her window and hop inside.

"Looks like you've done this before," I say.

"I have," she says plainly.

Veerka *definitely* isn't the same woman I remember. In the past, I'd always felt like her protector, and that excited me. But now, as I take in the woman standing before me—a tall, pale figure covered in black blood—I realize that she can handle herself just fine.

She'd probably put up one hell of a fight if we ever got into it.

The idea of her being dangerous kind of turns me on.

"Finish the job," she says coldly.

Seems she also likes to give orders now.

I can work with that.

Turning around, she unclasps her necklace and slides off her dress straps. When she faces me again, her dress slips off her body like butter in a hot pan.

Her collarbone, a smooth curve, makes me want to sink my teeth into her neck even though I'm not a vampire. Her breasts, round and perky, make me feel high.

My gaze makes its way to her toned belly, her smooth hips, and her perfectly trimmed—

"Alexis," she says.

She raises her sapphire necklace to my face, pulling my attention away from her body.

"Oh... right," I say.

Shaking my head to fight off the daze, I grab the sapphire and place it into the dead vampire's ashes.

254

Then, I bend down and pluck her dress from the floor and move it next to the necklace. As I make my way up, the tip of my nose grazes her bare inner thigh, and I find myself sucking in a lungful of her sweet scent.

Finish the job, Alexis.

Once everything is set over the ashes, I turn away from her and turn my camera back on.

"Jamieson, it's done."

When he remains silent, I tap my earpiece to make sure it's working. "Jamieson?"

"Y... yeah, I'm here. Holy shit, Alexis, you did it."

"Yeah, I did. And now I have to get the fuck out of here before Lucius comes back."

"Take the necklace." His voice is so cold I barely recognize him.

"Excuse me?"

"Take the necklace, Alexis."

I fucking hate being told what to do. Well, for the most part. When Veerka gives me an order, it's hot as hell. But from anyone else, I don't put up with that shit. And since when is Jamieson such an asshole with me? I've seen him be a complete prick with other people, but never with me. I guess Veerka was right. He's a shady guy, and he'll be nice to anyone who gives him what he wants. Right now, I'm standing in the way of what he wants. He could have played his smooth game and lured me in with some extra cash, but he's freaking out at the other end.

This necklace means something, and he's so scared of losing it he can't think straight enough to manipulate me.

"I already told you—"

"Get me that fucking necklace, Alexis, and then you get your money."

"Are you fucking kidding me?" I snap back. "That's not how this works. Send me the money—"

"The necklace, Alexis."

I reach into the ashes and pull out her necklace.

"Good girl," he says, and I grind my teeth.

"Send me the money, otherwise you'll never lay eyes on this thing again," I say.

He scoffs into my earpiece. "Do you seriously think I'm going to hand over five million dollars without getting what I want? I could easily cut you out of my life—"

"Yeah, you could," I cut him off. "But here's the thing, fuckface: if you don't pay me, I'm keeping this thing and selling it. It's probably worth, what, a million? Maybe two?" I'm playing stupid. The necklace is worth more than his payout, but if I play this right, I'll come out laughing. "I can live off a million bucks for a while. But obviously, this thing's more important to you than it is to me. So unless you send me the cash right away, you're never seeing this thing again."

He goes quiet. I must have struck a nerve.

Good.

"Three million," he says. "You'll receive the rest

of it when you deliver the necklace."

Fucking bastard.

"Fine," I say. "Send it now."

He goes quiet again, and I receive a notification on my phone:

Funds have been transferred into your account by ZeroAcct 0901241.

I know it's him, even though the account name changes every time he wires me cash. But to be on the safe side, I open up the notification. My new balance shows I'm three million dollars richer.

Sweet.

The only reason Jamieson gets away with transferring such enormous amounts of money is that he owns half the city. And with how much money the guy makes, transferring a few million dollars to a contractor isn't so farfetched.

Besides, on paper, I'm a *strategic consultant* to a multibillion-dollar company, and everyone knows consultants make a killing—pun totally intended.

"I expect that necklace to be delivered tonight–"

"Jamieson," I cut him off. He's silent long enough for me to pause for effect. "Go fuck yourself."

And with that, I tear out my earpiece and camera and crush them in my hands.

CHAPTER 31

"How is this going to play out?" I ask.

Veerka turns around with two glasses of wine in her hands. Handing one to me, she smiles. "To our new partnership."

I won't say no to booze. I grab it and gulp the whole thing down. She gives me a sour look that says, *Don't you have any class?* She knows I don't.

"Hold that thought," I say. With the empty glass pressed awkwardly in my elbow, I pull out my phone and shoot Drax a text:

Hey, it's me. All good. Give the witch her stuff back for me.

Then, I send another message to Rachel:

Go see Drax. You can have your stuff back.

Finally, I write a third message to Adrian, better known as Clock Dragon:

Meet me @ 28 Relik Ave in 4 hours.

I'll give him the one hundred thousand dollars I promised. All I have to do is reach out to Ouru to get that kind of money taken out without causing suspicion. Not only does he give me new identities when I need them, but he also has countless ways of creating fake bank accounts and moving money around without anyone noticing.

But right now, my priority is Veerka.

I slip my phone into my back pocket, glance up at her, and elevate my glass. She pours me another drink and says, "Do you have any idea how much this costs?"

"Do we care?" I say.

She smirks. "No, and we shouldn't. Lucius paid for it."

I cringe at the sound of his name.

"In addition to monthly payments, I'll cover the rest of your payout, Alexis."

I'm surprised to hear this coming out of her mouth. Why is she doing this? Does she want me as badly as I want her, or does she think I'm capable of helping her bring down Asmodeus?

"You don't have to do that," I say.

"I want to."

I find myself staring at her naked body again. She hasn't bothered slipping back into her dusty dress. I get the feeling she's toying with me; it's like she enjoys watching me get all worked up.

Watching me with a lifeless expression, she takes a sip of her wine and places the glass down on the vanity table. Slowly, she moves toward her bed with hips swaying from side to side and all I can do is look at her ass. When she reaches the edge of the bed, she sits down.

Her eyes remain fixed on me as she climbs backward onto her bed, taunting me.

Afraid to drop my glass of wine, I squeeze it, and it shatters in my hand.

"What are you waiting for, Alexis?" she says. "I'd like to celebrate our reunion."

She spreads her legs apart, and my jaw nearly unhinges.

I'm not sure what her big plan is for this partnership, but I don't give a flying fuck right now. I'm a multimillionaire and I have the girl I've always wanted. Taking down Asmodeus and saving the world can come after she does.

Wiping the shards of glass off my hand, I move toward her. "Let's fucking celebrate."

Visit **www.shadeowens.com** for more works by Shade Owens, including book 2 of this series – *Born to be Devilish.*